JUST LIKE GREY 8

CAMERON SPENCER

JESSIE COOKE

WWW.JESSIECOOKE.COM

CONTENTS

A Word from Jessie   v

Chapter 1	1
Chapter 2	7
Chapter 3	13
Chapter 4	19
Chapter 5	25
Chapter 6	31
Chapter 7	37
Chapter 8	43
Chapter 9	50
Chapter 10	56
Chapter 11	62
Chapter 12	68
Chapter 13	74
Chapter 14	80
Chapter 15	86
Chapter 16	92
Chapter 17	98
Chapter 18	104
Chapter 19	111
Chapter 20	117
Chapter 21	123
Chapter 22	129
Chapter 23	135
Chapter 24	141
Epilogue	147

More Books by Jessie Cooke   153

A WORD FROM JESSIE

Just like Grey is an Amazon Best Selling Series.

All books in the series are written for open-minded adults who are not easily offended, so you will encounter anything from cheating, explicit sex, unprotected sex, drug use, adult language, and many more topics that could upset the wrong reader.

These are not vanilla stories.

That said...I hope you enjoy it.

Happy Reading,

Jess

1

CAMERON

"Please, come on, you have to listen to me."

"No, I don't think I fucking do," I fired back, as I stormed out of my apartment and down the stairs. I didn't even know where I was going. All that I knew for sure was that I needed to be as far from here as possible, because if I stayed a second longer, I was going to lose my fucking mind.

I couldn't believe it. I was still sure, in some place at the back of my head, that this had to be some sort of mistake. Maybe a joke? But what kind of sick fucking joke would that have been – my fiancée, the woman I was meant to marry in a few months' time, giving head to the man who was supposed to be my best friend. My business partner. His dick in her mouth, right there in the middle of the living room that I had paid for. The image was already burned into my brain, and I knew it was going to take all the vodka in the world to get it out of there.

I tried to head for the door of the apartment building, intending on getting as far away from her as I possibly could, but she caught up with me before I could make it out on to the street outside. Planting a hand on the door to stop me going anywhere, she glared at me.

"You need to listen to me, Cameron," Adrienne repeated herself, voice sharper and harsher than before. She always got like this when she knew she had been caught out – acted as though she was the one trying to hold her anger in. But this time, I wasn't going to indulge this bullshit. There was no way she could spin this to me. I had seen her sucking Matt's dick, and nothing could un-suck that cock as far as I was concerned.

"Okay, I'm listening," I told her, turning and staring straight at her expectantly. "You want to tell me what the hell was going on there?"

She clearly hadn't thought this far ahead – she'd been ready to tell me to slow down, but not what to say to me when I actually did. She opened her mouth, closed it again, looked like a goldfish blubbing for air.

"So? I'm waiting," I prompted her. In truth, I just wanted to hear what she would say to me that she thought would even come close to passing off what she had just done with my business partner in the home that we were meant to be building a life in together. I still had to confront Matt about all of this, but at least he'd had the sense not to think that running after me was the best option. He knew me well enough to understand that he was simply better off getting out of there and hoping that he never ran into me again. Because if I got my hands on him...

"It wasn't what it looked like," she protested, the oldest lie in the book, and I rolled my eyes at her.

"Oh, yeah, right," I snorted back. "He was just deflating and you were blowing him back up, were you?"

"I didn't know what I was doing," she whined. "I – you have to believe me, I would never cheat on you..."

"Apart from the time that I walked in on you blowing my best friend," I replied. "Yeah, I appreciate that, but it's a gap in the story that I'm not willing to overlook, alright?"

"Where are you going?" she demanded, as I brushed her hand away from the door and pulled it open.

"I don't know," I shot back. "Nowhere that you can find me, that's for sure."

"Cameron, you need to stay, so that we can talk about this..."

"I don't need to do anything," I told her. And with that, I stepped out onto the street, and slammed the door hard behind me – loud enough that a couple of people passing by on the sidewalk gave me a hard look, obviously irritated that I had dared get in the way of their day.

Well, I didn't give a fuck. If they knew what had just happened to me, I was pretty sure that all these New Yorkers around me would have been willing to set the place on fire with the two of them inside. I just couldn't believe what I had seen – I was still trying to wrap my head around even a tiny part of it. It felt like I had been hit over the head with a big cartoon anvil, squashed flat onto the sidewalk below me. But no – I was still on my feet, and they had to take me somewhere, anywhere, that would get me as far away from the two of them as I possibly could be.

Adrienne had been cheating on me. I had wondered about it at the back of my mind for longer than I might have cared to admit, but I had always put that down to my own paranoia. I had been cheated on by my long-term girlfriend when I had been in college, and the thought of giving myself over to someone like that again had been enough to scare me into second-guessing every late night that she took out with her friends. But she had promised me, sworn up and down, that she would never do a thing like that to me. That she would never hurt me in that way. That she respected me too much to even think about being with someone else behind my back. She had always told me that if she had wanted someone else, she would have done the decent thing and broken up with me, but that she couldn't see that happening because she was just so in love with me.

Yeah, that had been a while ago now, that was for sure. Around the time that we got engaged last year. Looking back, I couldn't help but wonder how long it had been since she had last expressed a sentiment of such sweetness to me – a hell of a long time, that was for sure. Probably as long as she had been fooling around with Matt behind my back.

And Matt – for Matt to do this, that was maybe the worst part of all of it. A woman cheating on me, I had dealt with that before. But Matt Sawyer had been with me from the start, since we opened the PR firm that we ran together right out of college, and he knew how much I trusted him. He knew that I had put all this time and effort into building a life right beside him. We had always been able to be honest with one another, always spoken the truth, but now he had scarred me in the worst way that he possibly could, and I had no idea how I was meant to go back and fix the damage that he had done.

Shit. I wasn't sure that I could. I wandered the streets, not sure where I was going, bumping into people stupidly. It was the end of the workday – that had been where I was heading home from, from a meeting at the office that had wrapped up an hour early. Matt had known my schedule, which was likely why he had thought it was safe to head to my apartment to do whatever it was that he was doing with the woman who was meant to be my wife. Maybe he got off on doing it there, knowing that the two of them were sullying the home that I shared with her. Had they slept together on my bed? Ugh, I didn't even want to think about that, but I was pretty sure that I already knew the answer to it.

That was it. I was never going to let anyone new close to me ever again. It just wasn't safe. I had met Adrienne four years before, just after the business with Matt had started to really take off, and she had been the only woman I'd allowed into my life in a long time; apart from Alicia, of course, but she didn't count in the same way. I really thought that Adrienne was different. She seemed to be able to listen to my concerns, not to push me too hard on them. She had told me everything that I had wanted to hear.

But, looking back, that was because she was playing me for a total asshole. The fact that I had met her around the same time as I had really started bringing in big bucks was no coincidence. She had always wanted the very best of everything and felt no issues in making that much clear. She got with me because she thought that she could get the life she wanted by my side, not because she felt anything for me, that was for certain. Judging by the way that she had been going down on Matt, she was bolstering her chances, making sure that either of us would be willing to take care of her no matter what happened.

Well, now, I hoped that she had neither. I wasn't going to do a damn thing to help her out if I could avoid it. She had never paid a penny on that apartment that I owned – she had never even offered, in fact – and that ring on her finger would look better in the gutter, anyhow. She didn't deserve a single piece of it. She had made this bed, and now she could lie in it. Right alongside Matt, it looked like, since the two of them seemed so keen on each other.

I would have to deal with him at work, I knew that, but luckily I had a few days next week in meetings across the state – I wouldn't have to look him in the eye and hear his bullshit excuses quite so soon, much to my relief. He had always been the one out of the two of us who knew how to put a spin on any situation that would make it sound good, but there was no way in hell that he would be able to do that for this. I knew all his tricks, anyway, and I wasn't going to let him use them on me. Not a chance in hell. He had made his choice, and he was going to have to live with it. The two of them clearly deserved one another. They had betraying me in common, at least.

I eventually came to a halt when I noticed a bar that I had been to a hundred times before – a bar that I had used to visit all the time when I had been in college. It was a total dive, and looked like it hadn't moved far up in the world in the time that I had been doing the same, but maybe that was what I needed right now. Something that would take my mind off everything that was happening. Something that would allow me to go back in time and pretend that my life wasn't the giant shitshow that it felt like it was in that moment.

Alicia and I had used to come down here after classes together. Get a few drinks, get drunk, act as wingman and wingwoman for each other, respectively. And she was about the only person in my life right now who hadn't just pulled a three-sixty-dunk of a betrayal on me in the last forty-five minutes.

I grabbed my phone from my pocket, dialed her number, and waited a moment until I heard her on the other end of the line.

"Hello?"

"Hey, Leesh," I greeted her, using the nickname I'd always given her. "You'll never guess where I am right now."

2

ALICIA

AS SOON AS I SPOTTED HIM OVER BY THE BAR, MY HEART SANK.

I had seen my best friend Cam in a fair few states in his time. He had always been a guy who took things harder than most, more emotional than he would ever have admitted to being if he could avoid it. But now? Now, as he sat there on one of the cracked leather stools, it seemed as though he was about to slither off and onto the floor and just stay there, feeling sorry for himself.

I hurried over to him and gave him a quick hug as soon as I got the chance – he smelled of the expensive aftershave that he had worn since he was in college, even when he could hardly really afford to buy it. *You've got to look the part,* he always told me. And I would always shoot back, *What, and smell it, too?*

"I got down here as soon as I could," I told him, planting myself at the stool next to him and waving the bartender over to get us a couple of drinks.

"Thanks," he murmured, and he ran a hand through his usually impeccable dark hair – he looked as though he had recently crawled out from a bus crash. I had seen him hung over plenty of times before, since we had lived together for nearly three years, but this was something else entirely.

I picked up my drink as soon as it arrived and took a long sip of it as I looked at him. I sure as hell didn't like what I was seeing right now. This wasn't the Cameron I knew, that I had known all this time. He was more likely to talk me through my own emotional trouble than he was to have some of his own to bring to the table. Strong, comforting, those were the words that I had always associated with him. But now, I was going to have to step up to the plate.

Being back in this bar was a throwback, so much so that I was having to battle the feelings of déjà vu that were coming over me as I took a sip of the tequila-soda that I had ordered from the bartender. Smart's was still as much of a dive as it had ever been, and I could have sworn that some of the same patrons were sitting in the same dusty booths as when we had first made this our go-to watering hole. But that was the thing about having history with someone, I supposed – you couldn't unwrap all that history from that person, so much so that it got tangled up in your memories with the very person themselves.

And Cam and I had known each other for a hell of a long time. Since the first month of college, actually. Even though he had been doing business and I had been studying English Lit, we had ended up shoved together on a two-person quiz team for some icebreaker event at the local student union. The two of us had totally dominated and won the whole thing, and ever since that moment, we had been fast friends. We moved in together in our second year – just roommates – splitting the expenses for a tiny little flat above a Chinese restaurant that constantly smelled of soy sauce and oysters, and, since both of us had opted to stay in New York, we had remained part of each other's lives even since we had been able to get our own homes.

He was one of the most absurdly successful people I knew; if you wrote down everything that would make a person worthy of adulation in our society, then Cam had checked off each and every one on the list. He ran his own business, he'd made millions of dollars, he had a fancy fiancée who looked pretty in designer dresses on his arm at the big company events that they attended together. A beautiful apartment, a beautiful life, all of it.

Okay, and if I was being honest, maybe there was a little part of me that had always wondered what it would have been like to live that sort of lifestyle. It wasn't that I didn't find myself happy with my life, far from it, in fact – I wrote for a living, deliciously smutty romance books that didn't sell billions but brought in more than enough for me to live on. I had my little apartment, not far from Brooklyn, where all the hipsters and artists still made a point of congregating. I could cook more than just pasta from the packet, and I had a whole bunch of friends in the area who I knew would have dropped everything to help me out no matter what I needed help with.

But that didn't mean that I didn't look to him and wonder what it would have been like to live his life. To live in that gorgeous apartment with him, to be the beautiful woman on his arm who looked so perfect in designer dresses. I knew that I was hardly the girl who fit into that lifestyle so easily – I was loud, I talked too much, and the bits of me with curve were not the ones where curve was normally meant to lie – and even the knowledge of that wasn't enough to stop me wondering what it might have been like. Just for a little while. To live his lifestyle.

But as he sat there next to me, looking as though he wanted the floor to swallow him up, I got the feeling that things might not have been quite as idyllic as I thought they were.

"What's going on, Cam?" I asked him again. "Tell me, please. You sounded like a mess on the phone."

"Thanks," he replied, lightly sarcastic, and I managed a

smile.

"So, you going to fill me in?"

"Okay, look," he replied, and he sighed heavily before he spoke again, as though he could hardly believe that he was having to admit that this had happened at all.

"It's...it's Adrienne," he confessed, and my eyes widened.

"Is she alright?" I asked. Maybe she had been in an accident or something.

"Oh, she's fine alright," he replied, and there was a bitter note to his voice. "Doing really well, as far as I can tell. And I just walked in on her blowing Matt in our apartment."

My jaw *dropped*. I had written plenty of lines like that before in my books, but I had never actually had it happen to me in real life. But there was no other way to describe what the hell happened when he spoke those words out loud. I couldn't believe it.

"She was sucking his dick?" I exclaimed, loudly enough that a couple of people glanced around to glare at me. I wrote smut for a living; sometimes it was hard to remember that using that kind of language out in the real world didn't quite go down so well.

"Yeah, she was," he agreed, shaking his head, totally unfazed by my proclamation. "I can't fucking believe it. I thought that I could trust her, you know. I thought that I could really trust her..."

I pushed his drink into his hand quickly, and he took a long sip. He put the glass down with a clatter on the counter once more, and his head sank down on to my shoulder.

"Fuck, Leesh," he murmured. "What the hell am I meant to do now?"

"I don't know," I admitted. "But might I suggest getting totally drunk for the time being?"

"I think that's the best course of action," he agreed, and he lifted his head from my bare shoulder once more – I could feel the little scratch where the stubble had tickled my skin, and it sent a little shiver down my spine.

So we drank, and he talked, and he told me all about what he had seen – and the fact that his now-ex had had the nerve to go after him and tell him that he didn't understand what he was seeing and that he just needed to give her time to explain. I couldn't believe that she would really take him for that much of an idiot. She was the one who had been dating him all this time, she knew better than that, didn't she? I might never have thought much of Adrienne – a little too dull for my tastes, without many opinions on anything fun – but I had never taken her for stupid, that was for sure.

"So things are over with you guys now, right?" I asked, once he had filled me in on everything that had happened and just how he felt about all of it. I could hear the pain in his voice; I had been there when he had been cheated on by his college girlfriend, Georgia, and could vividly remember all the times that he had cried on my shoulder after one too many about never being able to trust someone again.

"Yeah," he replied. "I don't know if she knows that yet, but I sure as hell do. Why, you finally going to make your move?"

I parted my lips in surprise – I knew he was joking, but still. In truth, I had always thought that Cam was pretty cute, but I had long since put that to the back of my mind since we became friends and then roommates, and getting together would have just been more complexity than it was remotely worth. Too complicated for us to think about anything more than what we already had; a firm friendship that I wasn't going to let go anywhere.

"Or you got some girlfriends you want to set me up with?" he teased lightly. I let out a breath that I didn't realize that I had been holding, and grinned.

"Hey, you wish, buddy," I replied. "I'm keeping all my friends away from you, right? I'm not going to set them up with someone who thinks that this is an acceptable place to spend an evening."

"Fair point," he agreed with a chuckle, and he looked at his watch. "Shit, sorry, I didn't realize what the time was. Do you need to go meet with Jerry?"

I blinked at him for a moment, confused, and then I remembered – he had no idea that I had split with Jerry the week before. It had been such a non-event as far as I was concerned that I hadn't done the rounds to announce it or anything, just filling people in when they mentioned it. Jerry and I had been dating for almost a year, and he had been keen to make the move and finally start living together, but I had called things off before they went any further. I thought he was sweet, but I had no intention of spending the rest of my life with this guy.

But I didn't want to bring that up now, not when Cameron was right in the middle of his own hard time. He would shift all the attention to me and try to forget about his troubles, and that was the last thing he needed right now. So I shook my head.

"Nah, we don't have anything planned for tonight," I replied. "But you should probably get home soon. You don't want to wake up with a hangover tomorrow, right?"

"Yeah, probably not," he agreed, and he got to his feet and stretched. "How much do I owe you?"

"Nothing," I replied, and he opened his mouth to protest. I raised my hand to stop him in his tracks.

"I'm a rich, famous author now," I reminded him playfully. "I've got this, okay?"

"Well, I wouldn't want to let you down," he agreed, and I paid for our drinks. And tried not to let the little tipsy sensation prickle too much at the soles of my feet.

3

CAMERON

"You know, you just have to get back out there!" Mom exclaimed to me over the phone, as enthusiastic about my dating life as ever. I groaned and rubbed a hand over my face.

"Yeah, but I'm not exactly interested in getting back out there," I pointed out. "I only just *left* there. I don't think that I should be dating again so soon, not after what happened."

"Nonsense," she replied firmly. Mom had been planning to visit Adrienne and me over the weekend, so I'd had to give her a call to let her know that there was no way that it was going to happen. I'd gone for the PG story of what had gone down, but she had gotten the message. I was pretty sure she was glad to hear it, anyway. I knew that she had never had much time for Adrienne and had really just put up with her for my sake. And now that I was single, she had a long line of her friends' daughters that she wanted to set me up with.

"Okay, then do it with someone you already know," she suggested. "What about that nice Alicia girl? I always had a soft spot for her..."

"Leesh?" I replied, furrowing my brow. "Nah, she's dating

someone now anyway. Besides, we're friends, I wouldn't want to screw up what we have."

"Hmm," she muttered, and I could tell that she was already trying to find a way around that. My mom had never been one to back off even when I felt like she should have known better.

"She's my friend, Mom," I warned her. "Nothing's going to happen between us. I can tell you that for free."

"Yeah, I'll bet you can," she agreed, and I rolled my eyes, glad that she couldn't see me at the other end of the line. I was currently on the train, heading over to a meeting out of the city, glad that I was getting a break from the real world where all of this bullshit just seemed to insist on piling up in front of me.

I had officially broken things off with Adrienne as of the day before; I had taken a little time to think it over, once the drunk had worn off and the hangover had kicked in, but it hadn't taken long for me to make my mind up on what I wanted out of this. There was no way that I was ever going to be able to trust her again, and I wanted nothing more than to leave all of this behind me. She was a cheat, and the kind of cheat who enjoyed doing it with the worst person she could possibly think of. I wasn't interested in keeping her in my life. What was the point of being with someone who you didn't even know? It was bullshit. I had thought that I had a grasp on her all this time, but I had been wrong. I didn't know her at all. And the parts of her that I did, I wasn't even sure I liked that much anymore.

I could have kicked her out of the apartment, but in truth, I didn't have the heart for it. Besides, it wasn't as though I was just going to keep living there by myself, was it? Sit on the couch where I had walked in on her blowing my best friend. Or the person who *used* to be my best friend. I wouldn't be able to step foot in that place without thinking of the two of them together again, and that was the last thing I wanted to live my life trying to hide from. I had better things to do than torturing myself with the image of her sucking his dick. Though what better things, I wasn't quite sure yet.

Matt hadn't had the nerve to so much as come and talk to me since it had all gone down, pun fully intended. He had avoided the office as much as possible, and I got the feeling he wasn't going to make it easy for me to track him down even when he came back to work. It wasn't going to be long until people started to notice the fact that he was nowhere to be found, and when that happened, we were going to be in trouble. I didn't want anyone finding out about what had occurred out of the office. I knew that nobody would be able to look at me in the same way again, and the last thing I needed was the pity of the people who worked for me.

Matt usually dealt with them, to be fair, the people on the floors below us; he had always been the more outgoing between the two of us, the people person. I was the one who came up with the tactics and he was the one who executed them with a healthy dose of charm to make sure that everyone who was anyone was clamoring to work with us. And yeah, sometimes I looked at him and wondered if there wasn't a little bit of sliminess to the way that he conducted himself, but this was business; you had to be willing to be a little ruthless if you were going to achieve everything that you knew you were owed.

He had grown up in the city; I supposed that was the difference between us. I had just moved here for college when I had first decided that I wanted to work in the world of business. I was a small-town guy in a lot of ways, to the point where I sometimes had to put up those walls to make sure that I wasn't being taken advantage of. But I thought I had long since gotten past that place in my life, long enough past it that I wouldn't let something like this happen to me. That I wouldn't trust so easily again.

Mom, on the other hand, was still very much living that

small-town life. Even though Dad had passed away a few years ago, she still lived in the house that they had shared together, and I knew she was never going to leave that place if she got even half a chance. My sister, Freddie, lived down there still, and I made it back for all the big holidays. And besides, she could tell me how to live my life over the phone now, so she didn't have to worry about turning up in person to let me know everything I was doing wrong, did she?

"Oh, you know, Jackie's daughter just moved up to New York," she remarked, and I could hear some papers rustling at the other end of the line; sometimes, I teased her about having a file on me, and sometimes, I wondered if that wasn't so much a joke as it was a coping mechanism for the truth.

"Mom, I don't want to meet anyone new," I protested, but she had already breezed on past me to carry on with her announcements.

"I think you should just give her a chance," she replied. "Hope Langford. You remember the Langfords, don't you? They're a lovely family, you could do so much worse than her..."

"If I was looking at all," I muttered, but I knew that she was already halfway to making her mind up about this.

"I'll give you her number," she told me. "And I'll make sure that Jackie passes yours along to her..."

"If she's just moved here, I'm sure she's got a lot more to think about than dating," I pointed out.

"No, not at all," Mom replied brightly. "Besides, I don't think anyone would pass up the chance to go on a date with you, would they?"

"You're my mom, you've got to think that," I pointed out, and she chuckled.

"Yes, well, maybe you have a point," she conceded. "So, how are things going? Other than with Adrienne, I mean?"

I filled her in on everything else that had been happening in my life, and hoped that it would be enough to keep her off my back for the time being – but before I hung up, she made sure to remind me that she was going to pass along my number to that Hope girl, and that I should ask her out on a date.

"Right, sure," I replied, trying to get this over with. I knew that she would call to check in and follow up, and I tried not to think about it. We said our goodbyes, and I hung up the phone, then leaned my head to the window of the train and gazed outside.

I didn't know what the fuck I was doing wrong. I felt like I was a good boyfriend. Adrienne had agreed to marry me, for goodness' sake – she hadn't just done that out of politeness, right? Even if she had been fooling around behind my back, clearly the thought of spending the rest of her life with me wasn't so much of a problem for her. So what the fuck was I lacking that made the women in my life lose interest?

Well, the women I was dating, at least. Alicia had always been part of my life; even though we had met in college, it felt as though we had known each other for as long as we had been on this planet. She had been the one to turn out for me at the bar when I had needed her, even though she probably had plans with that Jerry dude she was still seeing – I didn't really get what she saw in him, but then, I wasn't the one dating him. She was.

Still. She could do better than that. Alicia had never had the best luck when it came to choosing the men to spend her time with; I had always teased her that it was because she expended all her romantic luck on those stories that she wrote, and the universe never had any left over when it came to her actual dating life. Jerry was a particular dud, in my opinion, a dull and slightly rude finance guy who liked to talk a big game about all the money he made, but never had any ideas of what he was actually going to do with it. Never a good sign. Still, if she was happy, then I wasn't going to get in her way.

Maybe I should have just gone for her in the first place. Before Adrienne, before Georgia, before any of this mess had started. Back when I had first met her, when she had been that slightly nervous college girl with the bright green eyes and the dark red hair and the skin that looked like vanilla ice cream. I could still remember the first time I laid eyes on her, before I knew what she would come to mean to me, when something inside me had leaned in and said *yes*.

But we had missed that boat now. She had moved on, and I had moved on, and the two of us were better friends than we were anything else. I didn't want to mess up what we had, not when it was so important to me – not when she was about the only person left in my life who hadn't taken it upon herself to hurt or betray me in some way. She was my best friend in the world right now, and I wasn't going to fuck that up.

My phone buzzed, and I looked down to see the message that Mom had followed up with – that girl's number. I sighed and grinned to myself. She meant well. And maybe she was right. Maybe I did need to get back out there. And maybe this girl was just the way to do that.

4

ALICIA

I sat back from my computer, stretched my arms over my head, and let out a satisfied sigh. Yes, that would do it.

I had been working since the moment I had gotten up that morning – I had a deadline to hit for my publisher, and I had promised myself that I was going to make up for the break from work that I had taken to help Cameron out with his issues. And now I was done, and I was pretty sure that this had to be one of the best entries in this series that I had ever pulled off in my life.

It had taken me a while to get these books off the ground, but now that they had, I knew that all my hard work had been worth it. They followed the exploits of a kinky self-made millionaire trying to find the woman of his dreams; mostly, my leading man, Andrew Fields, got caught up with models and actresses and socialites, but he was trying to find someone a little more grounded, someone who could handle the extent of his desires. Favorite outfit, a designer suit; favorite food, a boozy tiramisu. I knew everything about him. Every detail. Especially what he wanted most.

Enter Lana Waters; a smart, spunky journalist who writing a story on his company and finding herself caught up in his intense sex appeal. I was three books in now, real, print books, and I could still hardly believe that people actually wanted to *pay* for the stuff that I put out there.

A lot of the time I was growing up, I felt like I was an outsider. I had a dirty mind in a small town, and that wasn't something that people looked on too kindly when it came to women – we were meant to be demure and obedient and careful, not writing dirty fan-fiction about our favorite TV shows under a fake name so our parents couldn't track it down.

By the time that I left for college, I knew that I needed a bigger playground than the one I had grown up on. I loved books, and English literature was the closest thing I could find to diving into writing for my degree. That whole time, I kept writing; keeping a blog, filling it with anonymous recountings of my sexual exploits, as well as a few that I had just *wished* that I had been a part of. None of the college guys I had been with had been anything close to enough to fulfill my desires, and I had pretty much decided that exploring the kink in my writing was the closest I was going to come to experiencing it in real life.

It wasn't that I didn't like having sex. I loved it. I was good at it, too, if I did say so myself. But so many of the men that I had been with just couldn't seem to fulfill what I really needed from a partner, what I really wanted. Of course, they could spank, they could tie me up, they could call me a slut, but it never seemed to come from a real place inside of them. Their dominance lacked something, that zing, that certainty, that ability to take the control from me and make it feel like that was how it belonged. Jerry had been the worst at it, though he thought that he had been the best; looking back, his attempts to play sexy Dom were almost a little funny. I hadn't mentioned that to him, when I had done the dumping, but I was sure that my giggles at crucial moments had told him that I hadn't taken it seriously.

And so, I stuck to my books. Writing it was almost the same as doing it, right?

Plus, it gave me a lot of time to deep-dive into that side of sex and call it part of my job. People often asked me if I got turned on when I was writing this stuff, and every time I would laugh and shake my head and tell them that it was just work, but in truth, more than occasionally, I found myself overheating in front of my computer and having to take a little vibe-break to keep my head on task.

In fact, now that I was done, I couldn't help but notice the heat that had built between my legs this whole time. I had left it on a big cliffhanger, one that had come after a really intense impact play scene, and even the thought of being treated like that had made my entire body shiver with delight.

I rose from the seat and headed through to my messy bedroom – the covers were dangling half-off the bed, almost on the floor, and I reached beneath my pillow to grab out my faithful bullet vibrator. Flipping onto my back, I pulled the pillow over so that I could prop myself up, pushed down the zipper of my jeans, and clicked the button on the top of the little purple bullet so I could treat myself to a celebratory orgasm.

"Mmm," I moaned softly, as I felt it roll over my clit. The scene that I had just written, it had involved whips and restraints – Lana, bound to the bed, as her man lavished her body with attention, both pain and pleasure. I reached one arm above my head and closed my eyes, imagining that it had been me bound to that bed – imagining that I was waiting for my unfriendly neighborhood dominant to come and give me what I needed.

I wasn't sure what it was about the pain that turned me on. Maybe it was more about the control – the ability to totally detach from the way that I ran my life for a while. I had always been the girl who ran her life just the way I wanted, but that didn't mean that there wasn't a part of me that didn't want to let go for just a little while.

I rolled the vibe over my clit as I imagined him – the man, my man, standing over me. A whip in hand. Stripped to the waist, the rest of the suit that he had been wearing tossed to the floor behind him. Towering over me, looking down at me with those deep, brown eyes, not pulling his gaze from me for a moment.

"You want this?" he asked, as he reached out and trailed the leather tip of the whip over my hip. All I could do was nod.

"Say it," he ordered me, and I inhaled sharply, trying to find the words. Sometimes, when I was so lost to arousal, I found it hard to think about my actual words. But for him, I could speak it. I could say it out loud.

"Yes," I breathed, in my fantasy. And he didn't hold back for a moment longer.

Bringing the whip down on my thigh, he sent a judder of pain through my whole body. Even in my head, I could have sworn that I almost felt it on my skin, the pain of it shocking my system all at once. I had never had someone use a whip on me before, nothing other than a hand, but I knew that I would love it.

And, in my head, he did it again and again and again – he covered my body with welts of pain, sending red, raised marks all over my body. On my ass, my thighs, my outstretched hands, once he had untied me. Inside this little fantasy of mine, I could almost smell him; familiar, something that I knew, though in my fog of arousal and need I couldn't really focus on where it came from.

When he decided to fuck me, there was nothing that I could have done to stop him, not that I would have wanted to. I could almost feel his strong hands pushing my legs apart, and, even in the real world, I felt my thighs parting a little. The rush of the vibrator was almost painful in how good it felt, how close it was pushing me towards the edge. I had been keening for this all day long. Even though I would have preferred a real man, a real dick, I knew that the one I had invented in my head was the closest I was going to get to the satisfaction that I needed.

Back in my fantasy, he pushed my hands above my head, the skin still raw from where he had been whipping them, and told me to lift my hips off the bed. I did as I was told at once, too lost to what he was doing to me to argue. And, finally, *finally*, I felt the tip of his cock pressing at my needy slit, my pussy so wet that he could have slid into me in one thrust if he'd wanted to. But instead, he took his time. Watching me. Looking at me. Guiding himself into me, slowly, deeply, making me wait, knowing that I was hungry for him and that I couldn't stop myself mewling out with desperation...

I came, helplessly, crying out so loud that I wouldn't have been surprised if the neighbors had come banging on my door to make sure that someone hadn't broken in to kidnap me. My pussy pulsed against the vibrator, the clenching of my muscles sending waves of pleasure through my whole body – the hair on the back of my neck stood up, the tingles shivering down my arms and right to the tips of my fingers. It wasn't like I didn't spend a lot of time masturbating in this line of work, but that – that had been something special. I clicked the vibrator off and let it lie beside me, catching my breath and smiling at the ceiling. There was nothing like an orgasm to take the edge off a long day, that was for sure. Maybe I would even treat myself to another later on, after I'd had something to eat – ooh, I could order takeout, just spend the day in bed. That sounded good. I deserved to treat myself.

My eyes drifted shut, and I realized that I was exhausted. I had been up all day, since the sun had come up, working, thinking, writing, this one man running around and around inside my head until I wasn't sure if I had ever had room for anyone else in there at all. The only man who had been a constant in my life, given my miserable failure of a dating life.

I flipped over onto my side, hugging the pillow against my chest, and found him still playing in my brain. The way he looked, the way he tasted, the way he touched me, I knew it all so well that I could recite it all from memory. He was familiar to me, as though I had known him all my life.

And, as I lay there, all alone in my bed, something hit me. Something that instantly cleared the cache in my mind and demanded all my attention. And my eyes flew open at once.

That smell. The way he had smelled in my head. I knew it was just a tiny detail, but suddenly, it sent everything else slotting together in my brain. I knew that aftershave. It was...it was Cameron's.

Suddenly, and in a split second, the gaps were filling in inside my head. The suit on the ground in my fantasy, that had been the one that he had been wearing. His eyes, those eyes, they were the ones that he looked at me with when he was laughing at one of my jokes. That man, that man that I had invented as the very pinnacle of my sexual fantasy, I hadn't invented him at all. I already knew him.

And he was my best friend in the whole world.

5

CAMERON

"Hey, nice to meet you," the woman greeted me nervously, as she rose from the table that I had booked for us and extended her hand in my direction. I tried to bolster myself for what lay ahead.

"Hope?" I replied, and I took her hand. She nodded.

"Yeah, that's me," she agreed, and we both let out this nervous little chuckle. I still couldn't believe that I had allowed my mother to talk me into this. Christ, was I really that desperate to meet someone else? A blind date? It was hardly what I needed right now, but it was better than sitting at home alone all Friday night, I figured.

I noticed that Hope had a book sitting on the table, splayed open at the page she had been looking over when I had arrived. I picked it up and turned it around so that I could get a better look at the cover. And when I saw the name of the author, I couldn't help but smile.

"What are you grinning about?" Hope asked, tucking a strand of her short dark hair back behind her ear. "Are you a fan of hers, too?"

"No, I've never read any of her books, but I know her," I

replied, tapping the name on the cover. "Alicia Markle. She's a friend of mine."

Hope's eyes widened.

"No way!" she exclaimed, and she burst out laughing. "I'm such a big fan of her work. Can you tell her to hurry up with the next book already?"

"I'll see what I can do," I agreed, and the waiter came over to pour us a glass of wine. I took a deep breath and tried to cool myself off. This was going to be fine, wasn't it? I was just meeting this girl; nothing had to come of it. As Hope thanked the waiter and picked up the menu, I took a moment to check her out; she was pretty, but far removed from my type. Waif-like and slender, she was dressed in a smart, chic outfit that looked as though it could have come straight off any catwalk; her short hair flattered her small features, but it didn't do much for me. I didn't find myself fighting the urge to run my fingers through it. She glanced up at me, offered me a brief smile, and then returned her gaze to the menu.

No doubt she was giving me the same once-over. I had no idea what she was going to make of me. It had been so long since I had even thought about dating that I had no clue how I was going to come across. Was I meant to say something here? Did I tell her why I was so suddenly single again? No, I doubted that was the right idea. Shit, if only I had Alicia in my ear right now – she always seemed to know what women wanted, and she would have been able to guide me on this so I didn't make a total ass of myself.

"So, you're new to the city, huh?" I asked finally, after a long, slightly awkward silence as we looked over the menu.

"Yeah, I just got here," she replied. "But you've been here for a while, haven't you?"

"Yeah, I moved here for college," I said. "And then I started my business here and decided to stay."

"Oh, and what's your business do?" she asked with interest.

"Public relations," I replied. "I run it with my business partner, Matt. We've done pretty well out of it so far."

"Huh," she replied, and she eyed me for a moment.

"What is it?" I wondered aloud, but she shook her head.

"Nothing, nothing," she assured me. "What are you going to order? What looks good?"

I managed to keep the conversation going through the rest of the meal, though it was a bit of a strain and I hoped she couldn't tell just how hard it was having to try not to give in to my urge to just get up and go home. It wasn't her; she was a perfectly sweet girl, smart and witty, and I knew that any other man in this restaurant would most likely have been delighted to get a chance to share dinner with her. But I felt like every foot I put forward was just to tread on hers. I couldn't get into the pace of this, into the beat of it. And I was pretty sure that she could sense my discomfort right now, too.

The food was good – I had chosen the restaurant, figuring that I at least wanted a decent meal out of this even if the date turned out to be a bust – and she told me about flying in from out of state, what she planned to do now that she was here. I tried my best to tune in and listen, but honestly, I was having a hard time keeping my focus. I knew that this had been too soon for me to jump back into seeing someone, and I had proved myself totally right. I just hoped that this girl wasn't too mad at the fact that I was wasting her time.

But once I had taken the romantic part of it out of the equation, I managed to relax a little. Make some conversation. She was asking a lot about my work, about my life here, about my dating life, even – I just told her that I was single, and she asked what kind of woman I was looking for. I shrugged.

"I just want someone real," I replied, bluntly. Maybe it was a little too on-the-nose, but she had asked, and I wasn't going to lie to her. I needed someone who was going to look me in the eye and give me the truth, instead of dancing around it and trying to say what I thought she wanted to hear. She gave me that look again, the same one that she had given me when I had told her what I did for a living.

"I thought you might say that," she remarked, and she finished the last bite of her dish and took another sip of her wine.

"You want to get dessert?" she asked me, once the main meals had been cleared away. Before I so much as had a chance to answer, the waiter had returned with dessert menus, and I grinned.

"Well, I think that choice has been made for us," I replied. I knew what I was going to get before I even glanced at the menu.

"What are you having?" she asked, and, before I could answer, she lifted a finger to stop me.

"Wait, let me guess," she told me. "Tiramisu?"

I furrowed my brow at her, totally thrown by the fact that she seemed to be able to read my mind.

"How did you know?" I asked, and she shook her head and let out a long sigh. She reached into her bag and pulled out the book that I had noticed when I had first arrived.

"Because it's all right in here," she told me, and she pushed the book across the table towards me. I shook my head.

"I don't know what you're talking about," I replied, and she flipped the book open, taking a second to skim through the pages before she landed on what she was looking for.

"See, here?" she pointed out, and turned the book around to face me, finger stabbing at a particular paragraph on the page. I read what was in front of me – sure enough, it was a small scene of a man ordering the very same dessert that I had been planning to have.

"Okay, I don't see what that's got to do with me, though," I protested. "Just because it turned up in a book that you were reading..."

"Don't you see, it's not just this," she replied. "The guy in this book – Andrew Fields – he's *you.*"

I almost burst out laughing at her declaration. It just sounded too crazy to me to even entertain it for a second.

"What are you talking about?" I asked, shaking my head as I handed it back to her. She put the book back in her bag, tented her fingers, and began talking quickly, as though she had to get this whole theory out of her head before her brain exploded.

"I've read all of this series so far," she explained. "The whole thing. And Andrew Fields, he's seriously just you. He runs the same kind of business, he came from the same kind of place – he even says that he's looking for the same kind of woman that you are. I'm pretty sure he wears that exact suit that you have on in one of the scenes in this one, too. Trust me, I know these stories inside out, and I'd recognize the leading man if I saw him."

"And you think you see him?" I muttered. I couldn't make sense of any of this. Was Hope just a little crazy? Or was she on to something?

"You were going to order that dessert, weren't you?" she remarked, as she pointed to the menu. "The tiramisu."

I nodded. And she leaned back from the table and held her hands up, as though to tell me that the case was as good as closed.

"Then I think that seals it for me," she replied. "You're him. And I don't know if you're just trying to act like him because you know women like it, but if you are, that's seriously the saddest thing I've ever heard in my life."

"I'm not trying to act like anyone," I replied defensively. "I told you, I've never read those books before in my life. I didn't even know that guy's name before you told it to me right there."

She cocked her head to the side and looked at me for a long, quiet moment. And then, she grinned.

"Then I think you might have some talking to do with that friend of yours," she remarked. "Because, whether she knows it or not, she totally wrote you into her books as some sort of sex god."

My jaw dropped, and I had to stem the bubble of laughter that wanted to bust out of my mouth as soon as she said that.

"No way Alicia meant it like that," I replied, shaking my head. "No way."

"I'm just saying," Hope replied, holding her hands up. "So, do you want to get that dessert, or...?"

We finished up our meal with something sweet, and I paid and thanked Hope for her time. My head was spinning. Could she be right about Alicia? About her books? About...about me?

"I get the feeling we're not going to be doing this again anytime soon," Hope remarked, and I smiled apologetically.

"If you need a friend in town, you can always hit me up," I offered to her. "But I think I have some stuff to figure out before I think about dating again."

"Tell me about it," she replied, and she gave me a kiss on the cheek and pulled on her coat. "But thanks for tonight. I appreciate the company."

"Yeah, safe journey home," I muttered. But in truth, my mind wasn't on her anymore. It was on Alicia. On those dirty books that she wrote for a living. And the fact that, apparently, the sex god of a main character might just have been me.

I knew I had to talk to her about this. And I wasn't willing to wait. I flagged down a cab outside the restaurant and gave the driver her address. I needed her to look me in the eye and tell me that this wasn't true. Or – even better – that it was.

6

ALICIA

"Leesh, I know."

As he stood there in the doorway to my apartment, dressed for a date and looking hotter than hell, I tried to get my head straight and work out just what he was saying to me.

"Cameron, I don't know what you're talking about," I fired back, but he must have been able to tell that I was lying. I didn't know how he had figured it out – maybe I had beamed it into his brain from afar or something like that – but he knew, and there was no denying the fact that this was really happening, whether I wanted it to or not.

"Yes, you do," he replied firmly, and he stepped over the threshold and closed the distance between us, pushing the door shut behind him. "You know what I'm talking about, don't you, Alicia?"

When he used my full name, and not the shortened version that he always called me, I knew that something serious was going down. I opened and closed my mouth, not sure how to respond to any of this now that it was right in front of me.

"I don't know..." I tried to repeat myself, but he shook his head, began to stride around the apartment. I wished I could have stopped him, but he had every right to be as mad as he was in that moment. If he had worked out what I thought he had worked out.

"I was on a date tonight," he told me, finally turning to look at me. I couldn't tell what the expression on his face was meant to convey to me, but I got the feeling that it was close to anger. There was something else to it, though, something underneath that – I wanted to uncover it, to reach in and discover it for myself, but I wasn't sure what he would do if I took another step closer to him.

"And she told me that I was pretty much playing the part of the leading man in your romance books," he continued. "She thought that I was making some kind of joke at her expense, until I told her that I'd never read them, and that you were the only connection that I had to them. And frankly, I'm not sure what I'm meant to do to get my head around that, Alicia. You care to help me?"

He was staring at me now, as though he was daring me to shoot back with something smart. But in truth, I had nothing smart left in my head at that moment. Nothing that would have come close to explaining the mess that I had made when I had put him in my book. I didn't even know how it had taken me so long to figure out that it really was him – I spent so much time with that character, almost every day of my life, and yet I hadn't been able to work out that he was standing right in front of me every time Cameron and I met for drinks?

"I didn't know what I was doing," I confessed, quickly, getting the words out of my mouth as soon as I could. I needed to protect myself. Protect our friendship. Because he had every right to be mad at me. And I needed to find some way to make it right once more before he stormed out of here for good, and refused to see me ever again.

"What are you talking about?" he replied, and he sounded –

okay, there was a hint of exasperation to his voice, but there was more to it, too. More to what was going through his mind, for sure. I could tell that he was curious. I had known him long enough to be able to read into his brain, to be able to tell when there was some part of him that wanted to know more. This was one of those times, I was sure of it. It might have been difficult for me to put it into words for him right now, but I knew that he wasn't going anywhere.

"I really didn't even think about the two of you in the same sentence until really recently," I went on. "I knew that...well, I knew that the character, he was just some kind of archetype, and I wanted to base him on a man that I actually knew and liked, and I guess that you've been the only consistent example of that in my life, so he just got attached to you in my head and then..."

I trailed off again. I felt like my breath was tearing out of my lungs as he looked at me. His eyes were dark, an expression that I had never seen on his face before. – but one that I had seen on the face of the man that I had based on him, in my mind's eye. This was just what he looked like before he...

"And then?" he prompted me. I realized that I had left the sentence unfinished.

"And then, I had written the books and people like them so I just decided that it was easier for me to go along with it than think about changing him. You, I mean," I finished up. "I know I should have told you, but you never wanted to read them, anyway, and it's not like millions of people look at them every day. The chances of you ending up on a date with someone who's actually read the series was so slim..."

I kept on running out of words to soothe him. There was something about the way that he was looking at me that was making it hard to think straight. It was as though the man I had written all this time, the man I had come up with in my head to fulfill all my wildest fantasies, as though he had blended with my best friend and now I was trying to find the space between them and coming up with a hard blank. They were just one and the same now, and I didn't know if I could tell the difference any longer. And that, I knew better than anything else, was a dangerous place to be.

"You wrote me into that series," he spoke, finally, voice low and considered, as though he was choosing every single word out of his mouth as carefully as he could.

"And you made me some kind of...some kind of sex god?" he finished up. Finally, I could see a little smile play at the corner of his lips, and I felt a wash of relief pass over me. There was no worse feeling in the world than the sensation that your best friend was mad at you. I nodded, and bit down on my lip.

"I know it's crazy," I conceded. "Really, I get that, I do. And if I could go back in time and figure it out earlier, then I would have done something to change that. But I just...you're the only man who's ever been a constant in my life, Cameron, and so you just became the stand-in for him."

"Yeah, I get that," he replied. "Because it's not like we've ever had sex, is it?"

I parted my lips – the way he was phrasing that question, it was almost as though he expected me to contradict him, but the two of us had never gone to bed together. Okay, it had crossed my mind a couple of times, but never in any sort of serious way. Just...a wondering, I supposed. Not a question.

"Yeah, of course," I replied, and I felt a little heat run up the side of my neck. I hoped he couldn't see it. If he did, he might think that going to bed with him was something I actually wanted, and I was – well, okay, I wasn't certain that I didn't want that right now, since I had figured out that I had based my fantasy man on him, but I didn't want him thinking that. I had already come close enough to hurting our friendship with what I had done, and I had never wanted to do anything that might cause him to drop right on out of my life. If he never wanted to speak to me again after this, then I would have understood completely. How could he forgive me for turning him, or some version of him, into a masturbatory fantasy for the women who read my books? I had no idea how I would feel if someone had done the same to me.

"Because writing me into your books like that," he continued, and he took a step towards me. "A lot of guys would take that to mean that you had other things in mind for me."

My pulse started to pick up. I couldn't tell whether he wanted me to deny it or not. What was I supposed to tell him? I could smell his aftershave, that masculine, classic scent that seemed to swim around my head, to make everything a little more blurry around the edges.

"Some guys," he went on. "Some guys would think that you were hoping that I would be that man for you."

"They would," I agreed, trying to keep my voice as neutral as possible.

"I know what's in those books, Alicia," he continued. "I know the sort of stuff you're selling. And I don't know if that's what you want from me, or if that's some other mess in your head. But I need to know that you know what you want from me right now."

And, as he looked back at me, his eyes were dark and his gaze steady. And finally, as though it just couldn't be contained any longer, I felt something give inside of me.

I wasn't sure who moved towards the other first – all I knew was that within seconds, the two of us were kissing, and that it felt like it was setting off fireworks behind my eyes. His hands came to my arms, gripping them tight, and he pulled me against him as though this was all that he had been able to think about since the moment he stepped through the door. I slid my arms around his shoulders as I felt his tongue part my lips, deepening the kiss, his rough stubble against my cheek, and I tried to remind myself that this was really Cameron. This wasn't my fantasy guy. This was my best friend. Though I wasn't sure that I could discern much space between them anymore.

He pushed me back against the door, let out what sounded like a growl against my lips, and it was almost like something inside me had liquefied; I wanted him so badly that any sense I had been hanging on to seemed to vanish all at once. I pushed my hands through his hair as I felt his fingers against my waist, pushing up the bottom of the light tee I was wearing so that he could feel my cool skin.

His teeth caught on my lip, and the sharp rush of pain pulled me back into my body for a split second. I tugged myself back from him, looked him in the eye, and tried to remind myself that this was reality – that this wasn't just one of the fantasies that I laid down in print every now and then to make my rent. His hands on me, his mouth on mine, this was really happening.

"Are you sure?" I managed to breathe to him, my head too much of a mess to think about getting out anything more coherent. And, instead of bothering with an answer, he just leaned forward and kissed me again. Any doubts in my mind vanished, as I kissed back the man I had been turning into fantasy all this time.

7

CAMERON

I PUSHED HER ARMS ABOVE HER HEAD, BRUSHING MY LIPS OVER HER neck, and felt the pulse of her heartbeat beneath my mouth. A reminder that she was here, that we were really doing this – that there was no denying the chemistry between us.

I heard her moan beneath me, and moved my mouth back around to meet hers, so that I could kiss her again. I couldn't get over how damn good it felt to just kiss her like this – it had been so long since I had made out with someone new, and I was sure that it had never felt as good as this. It was a clash of the newness and the familiar, the fact that this girl was my best friend and that I had known her all this time along with the fact that I had never touched her this way in all my life. I could feel her wrists straining against my hand, and I let them go so that she could touch me.

"Fuck," she gasped, as she reached down to unbutton my shirt – her fingers were shaking so much that I could tell she wasn't going to be able to do anything with them, so I brushed her hand aside and took over myself. She kissed me again, right on the corner of the mouth, and gazed at me with hunger in her eyes that told me she had been waiting a hell of a long time for me to catch up with her on this one.

I still couldn't believe it. She had really written all those dirty stories about me. She might have told me that it was just some version of me, but Hope had been so sure that the person in those pages was actually me, and I was struggling to get my head around it. She had really concocted all those kinky adventures, and, at the back of her mind the whole time, I had been there? The thought of her wanting me all that time, whether or not she had even been aware of it – it was stirring something in me that I'd had no idea I was hanging on to until that moment, and I liked it.

She slipped her hand down between my legs and gripped my cock through my pants – squeezing gently; I saw her tongue trace out a shape over her bottom lip, as though she was thinking about tasting me.

"I want to feel you inside of me," she murmured, and I kissed her again, harder this time, hoping that she would take that for the promise that it was. I pushed my hand down the front of her loose pajama pants, rubbing my fingers against the outside of her panties, and she let out another helpless moan of delight, as though she was already imagining what they would feel like inside of her.

"Turn around," I ordered her, and I left no room for argument in my voice – luckily, she wasn't putting up a fight, and she turned around at once.

I sank to my knees behind her and pulled down her pants and panties. I knew that we had firmly overstepped the line that any best friends could claim to respect now. Her ass was perfect, soft and curvy, and I couldn't resist leaning forward and planting my lips against it, baring my teeth against her flesh.

"Oh," she groaned, and she reached back to trace her fingers through my hair. She was vocal; I liked that. I supposed, given her line of work, it would have been strange if she was reticent about any of this. I bit down a little harder, and this time earned a squeal of pleasure from the woman above me.

I pushed her legs apart a little further, and I wondered where this guy had come from. I had never been the most aggressive when it came to sex, but there was something about this and her and everything that it represented that just seemed to draw it out of me. I wanted to hear her reactions, wanted to know that she was helpless to resist me. The thought of her sharing me for so long with her readers without me knowing a thing about it – sure, it turned me on, but I think I was within my rights to let it make me a little mad, too. And maybe that was what this was about – showing her that I was more than just a fantasy. That I was a real-ass man on top of that.

"Spread your legs," I commanded her, and she planted her feet a few inches wider. I could see that her pussy was already glistening with wetness, and I wondered if it had been for me from the moment I walked through the door. She told me she had been working on her new book; it made perfect sense that she would have been getting wetter and wetter, sitting at her desk, grinding helplessly against herself as she wrote up all these filthy stories about a man who was meant to be me.

I could smell her sweet, musky wetness, and I knew that I wasn't willing to wait to taste it from her – leaning forward, I stroked my tongue from her clit to her slit, grasping hold of her thighs as I did so, and felt her whole body shudder in response.

"Fuck," she groaned, and she planted her hands against the door for support, as though she might have just slumped to the ground without it there to support her. I went again, flattening my tongue, taking my time, watching the way she reacted, feeling the tense and release in her muscles. I wanted to make her come. I wanted to feel her come. I wanted to make sure she knew how it felt, to be helpless.

I pressed my mouth to her pussy and started to eat her out as though it was the only meal that I would be allowed all month. She was silky-smooth, freshly waxed, soft and musky and everything that I wanted from her. It didn't take long before she was grinding her hips back against my face, her breath starting to tear out of her lungs harder and faster than it had before. I tightened my grip on her thighs, sinking my fingers in, knowing that they would leave marks and not much caring if they did. I wanted to remind her what she had done, what we had done together. I didn't want the memory of this to fade as soon as it was over.

"Oh my God," she gasped, and I could tell from the ragged edge to her voice that she was getting close. I pulled my mouth back, looked up at her, and she gazed down at me, her eyes full of a pleading, keening longing that was almost enough to make me laugh.

"You close?" I asked her, and she nodded. With that, I rose to my feet, unzipped my pants, and took my cock in my hand.

"I want to feel you come," I told her, as I grabbed the condom I had rather hopefully packed for my date and sheathed myself with it swiftly. I needed to feel her around me. I needed to feel that perfect pussy on my cock.

"Fuck me," she mewled, the needy edge to her voice almost funny if it hadn't been so fucking hot to me. I wasn't sure what it was about this woman wanting me so badly that made me so hard, but, as I eased myself inside of her for the first time, I let out a sigh of release as the tension I didn't even know I had been hanging on to began to fade.

"You feel so good," I murmured into her ear, looping one arm around her waist and pulling her back towards me, the other on her hip so that I could control the depth of my thrusts. She was warm and wet and tight and welcoming – I couldn't remember the last time that I had fucked someone like this, fucked someone because it felt like I couldn't do anything but fuck them. I pressed my face to her hair, inhaled the scent of her greedily, and listened to those soft little moans she made every time I drove myself up to the hilt inside of her. I knew that she wanted this. She was greedy for it, just the same way I was. Neither of us could stop ourselves, could hold back, could even think about slowing down.

It didn't take long before she had arched her back to push herself back against me, grinding herself onto me as though she needed it as badly as I did. I was buried all the way inside her, right up to the hilt, feeling the pulse of her pussy around my full length every time I drove myself into her.

I took one hand in mine, guided it between her legs, and pressed it against her clit. I wanted her to take herself over the edge. She half-turned her head, and I kissed the corner of her mouth again, knowing that I would take any chance that I could get to just kiss her, taste her. To remind myself that this really was the woman I had known all this time.

"Come for me," I ordered her. I would never have given such a bold command before, but there was something about her that drew it out of me. I didn't have to worry about making a fool of myself because she was my best friend, and I knew that nothing that I said here would be enough to stop her caring for me. We had already seen each other in every state, and we still loved one another. Nothing was going to change that now.

It didn't take long until she let out this long, helpless cry of relief, as though her whole body had been keening for this since the very moment that I had walked through the door – she tightened around me, once, twice, again, and I held myself deep inside her, letting the sensation pulse through me, as though the pleasure was passing from her body to mine. And, moments later, I reached my own release buried deep inside of her, my cock twitching as I finally came, my face pressed to the back of her neck where her hair was tickling my skin. I planted a kiss on the nape of her scalp, and slowly pulled back.

By the time that we had both come back down to earth, and I had pulled out of her and disposed of the condom, there was a small smile on her face as she leaned back against the door. She looked sated, I was pleased to note, as though she had gotten just what she had been looking for.

"I can't believe that really just happened," she murmured, and I planted myself on her couch and gazed up at her for a moment. I knew how she felt. There was so much that I wanted to ask her in that moment – if it had been good for her, if it had lived up to everything that she had been hoping it would for all these years, if I was as good as she wanted me to be, if her boyfriend knew about this, if I should have been worried about what he might have had to say about it.

But, in that post-coital glow, there was only one thing that I could think of to reply to her. And so, I looked up at my best friend, and offered her a smile, hoping that she would be able to give me the answers that I was looking for right now if I only gave her one question to work with.

"So," I told her, raising my eyebrows. "What happens now?"

8

ALICIA

As I sat there in the coffee shop, waiting for him to arrive, I felt like I was going to explode from sheer nervousness.

What the hell was I going to say to him? I had no idea what I was meant to say, do, think, feel – none of that was clear to me yet. And, despite that, I had agreed to come along down here to talk it all over with him, so that the two of us could make sense of whatever the hell had happened between us when he had come around to my apartment a couple of days before.

The sex had been – well, it had been fucking incredible, if I was being honest with myself. I didn't know if it was just the taboo of hooking up with someone I had known so well for so long or if it ran a little deeper than that, but frankly, I didn't give much of a damn either way. All that I knew was that I had come harder than I ever had with anyone else in my life before, and that I was already craving a replay of our adventure together.

But was it the right thing to do? I had no clue whether or not I should have been pulling away from the very thought of more. I liked being with him – sexually, socially, all of it – but we were best friends, and I wasn't sure that I was willing to put that on the line for some more excellent fucking.

Which was why, when he had asked me what happened next, I had suggested that we take some time to think about it before we came to any quick conclusions. We'd agreed to meet here, a couple of days later, once we'd had a little space to get our heads straight. Except my head was still as much of a mess as it had been right after this had all happened in the first place, and I knew that nothing in the world was going to get me feeling normal again.

But when he finally walked in, I felt my heart flip in my chest, and a huge smile spread across my face at once. I couldn't help it. It was like a learned response at this point, something that had just been built into me because I loved being around him. I got to my feet and waved, and he smiled back and came over to join me. He was dressed-down, out of the date-night suit that he had been in when he had come to my place last, and looking like a whole-ass snack in a light gray tee and a pair of jeans.

"Hey," he greeted me, and I stood there for a moment, not sure how I was meant to respond – did I lean up and plant a kiss on his cheek? Give him a high-five? All of this was so new to me, and I needed to find some way to wrap my head around it.

"Hey," I finally offered in response. "Thanks for coming today. I thought you might change your mind or something."

"I don't think you'd let me get away with that," he remarked, the flicker of a smile passing over his lips.

"You have a point," I giggled. Why was I giggling? I felt like I was some sort of giddy schoolgirl. I was sure that I could feel the soles of my feet tingling against the ground beneath me. I took a seat and picked up the coffee I had been sipping on, and tried for the life of me to work out what to say next.

"So," he began, finally, and I thanked God that he had the nerve to launch into this first.

"So," I replied. "What are we going to do now?"

"Okay, first things first, I have to know," he replied. "What's going on with you and your boyfriend?"

"My ex," I corrected him, and he tipped his head to the side, clearly confused.

"I thought you guys were still together?"

"We broke up last week," I admitted. "I was going to tell you, I really was, but then everything happened with you and I didn't want you think that I was just piling on with what was going on in my life."

"You hid that from me?" he replied, furrowing his brow, and I shook my head.

"I was going to tell you, I promise," I assured him. "But you were going through enough without having to handle that too."

He smiled at me, clearly touched.

"Okay, you know you're the best friend I could ask for, right?" he told me, and I spread my hands wide like I was pulling off a magic trick.

"Oh, I know," I replied.

"Apart from the bit where you put me in your books and I didn't find out about it till I was on a date," he remarked, and I winced.

"Yeah, I guess I deserved that," I admitted. "And I'm sorry. I honestly – it didn't click with me until recently that it was you I was writing about, and I would have told you about it, but you never read those books anyway and I thought you might have thought that I was just overstepping the line."

"Yeah, well, I guess I'm glad that I know now," he replied. "Maybe I should actually get around to reading them, huh?"

"Maybe you should," I teased back.

"Then I can find out what you've been getting me up to in your books all this time behind my back," he went on, and I bit my lip. Honestly, even though I'd actually had sex with this guy now and everything, there was still some part of me that felt a little shy about the thought of him delving into my head in that way.

"I know I should have told you," I blurted out. "And I'm sorry it ruined your date and everything..."

"I think I had a much better night by the time it was all wrapped up," he replied, and I saw that flicker of amusement in his eyes, as though he could see the overheated red flush on my cheeks.

"So, we really did that, huh?" I remarked, finally finding the boldness to come out and confirm what I knew to be true.

"Yeah, we really did," he agreed. "And I think I'd like to do it again sometime. If you're down for it."

"Really?" I replied, eyes widening. I didn't know why, but I'd had it in my head that this was just something that was going to be forgotten by the both of us; something that we both put down to a little overheated tension at a time when the two of us had been through breakups. But here he was, telling me that he didn't want it to be over? Okay, now he had my attention...

"Yeah, really," he replied. "I've been thinking about it. I've just come out of a long-term relationship. I don't really feel like dating. And you're in the same place, right?"

"Yeah, more or less," I agreed.

"And I figured, well, if you've been basing all this writing off me all this time, then I might as well give you something to work with, huh?" he continued, and he grinned at me.

"You're offering to help me inspire my books?" I remarked, and he nodded.

"Not that I'll be expecting a co-writing credit, but you know, if it helps you out," he replied, as though he was doing me a great favor. I laughed.

"Oh, yeah, out of the goodness of your heart, right?" I giggled again.

"Anything for my best friend," he remarked, and that's when it hit me – this flirting was all in good fun, until it got to the point where it got in the way of our friendship. I chewed on my bottom lip and wondered if he had considered that as part of this deal that he was proposing.

"So, what about...us?" I replied. "I mean, I know that we're friends, but if we start sleeping together, does that automatically make us...dating? Or something?"

"It doesn't make us anything that we don't want to be," he assured me. "I know that I'm not looking for anything serious right now, but being with you was some of the most fun I've had in a long time. I don't want to give that up. Do you?"

"No, I really don't," I admitted. "So what would that makes us? Friends? With extras?"

"With benefits," he corrected me. "Hey, I thought you made a living writing about this sort of thing – shouldn't you know better?"

"Hey, stop getting up in my business," I fired back. "This is my world, remember? And who knows, if you piss me off, I could write you into a book in a way that's way less flattering..."

"Well, then, I'm just going to have to make a case for you to keep me in a good light," he replied, and beneath the table, I felt our knees pressing together. I could feel my palms getting a little sweaty, the fuzz of excitement dulling the corners of my vision. It was like he was the only person sitting in that room with me, as though everyone else could have just faded away into nothingness as far as I was concerned. How had I never noticed how gorgeous he was before? Okay, yes, I had *noticed,* but it had never made me feel the way that it was making me feel at that moment. As though it was meant for me. I wanted to reach out and rub my fingers along his jaw, to feel the roughness of his stubble beneath my fingers once more...

"So, we have a deal, then?" he asked me, and I laughed.

"You know I don't work for you, right?" I teased. "This isn't one of those board meetings you can take minutes at and go over later."

"You're right," he agreed. "You're way more interesting than anything like that."

But still, he stuck his hand out to me over the table and raised his eyebrows at me pointedly.

"But do we?" he asked with interest. "Have a deal, I mean. We keep this casual, but have some fun? Does that sound good to you?"

I looked down at his hand for a moment and was suddenly reminded of how it had felt when it had been between my thighs, pressing up against my panties. I slipped my hand into his without another moment's pause.

"It sounds perfect to me," I replied. "One thing, though – if either of us feels like it's going to get in the way of our friendship..."

"Then we call it off, no questions asked," he promised me. "You know that I don't want anything to get in the way of that, Leesh."

He was back to using his nickname for me again, and the sound of it coming out of his mouth was enough to put a smile on my face. Okay, so some things had changed, but his name for me had stayed totally the same. It held a casual, simple intimacy that made my heart warm, and I knew it always would.

"Neither do I," I agreed, and I leaned back in my seat. "So, does this mean that I have to pay for breakfast now? Or do you cover all the bills now that we're not-dating?"

"I think we're still going to split it fifty-fifty," he remarked, and he waved over the waiter to order himself something to eat.

Suddenly, I realized, I was ravenously hungry too. I had been ignoring my appetite all this time, but now that we had made our deal, it was like it had come flooding back to me all at once. And there was no way in hell that I was going to deny myself a chance to indulge.

9

CAMERON

"Hey, Cameron?"

I looked up from the book that I was reading, and, to my surprise, saw the last man on earth I was expecting to see right now.

"Matt," I muttered, as I tucked the book back into my bag and looked at him. "What are you doing here?"

"I...I wanted to talk to you," he admitted, and he fidgeted as he stood there in front of me, as though he was waiting for me to invite him in. I didn't say a word. If he wanted to speak to me, then he was going to have to make the effort to close the gap between us, since he was the one who had put it there in first place.

"You need me for something?" I replied coolly. I hadn't seen him properly since I had walked in on the woman I was meant to be marrying sucking his dick in my apartment, and, honestly, I had half-expected him to just quit his work here altogether. It was obvious that he couldn't stand to be in a room with me right now, no matter how much he might have liked to pretend differently, and I had no idea how he intended to navigate around the issue before us.

"I wanted to tell you that I'm leaving the city for a while," he replied, still standing rigid, as if he had been rooted right down to the ground in front of me.

"Where are you going?"

"The offices in Jersey," he replied. "I think it'd be better if I got some space from here for a while. And if you got some...time. To process everything."

"Yeah, of course," I answered. If he had come to me a week before, I would have turned him right on around and marched him out of there, but today, I was feeling a little more generous. Perhaps because I had spent most of the night before in Alicia's bed, reminding myself of just how good it felt to be with someone who really wanted me.

"You're not...are you still mad?" he asked me, and I got to my feet, made my way over to the door, and closed it behind him.

"Matt, what the fuck do you think?" I replied with another question. "How do you think I feel that you've been hooking up with my fiancée behind my back? How would you feel about it, if you were in my shoes?"

"I know that I shouldn't have done it," he confessed. "But she was always the one coming on to me, man, you have to understand that. I tried to call it off so many times, but then she would come by and she would just..."

"Okay, Matt, I saw the two of you together," I reminded him. "It didn't look much to me like you were fighting her off. I know what you guys did to me. I've come to terms with it, and yeah, I think it would be a good idea if you got out of here for a while, huh?"

"Yeah, you're right," he agreed, and he scuffed his foot on the floor, looking with every passing second more like an errant schoolboy who had been caught smoking under the bleachers.

"And I wanted to tell you," he went on, speaking faster now, as though he knew that his time in here with me was pretty fucking limited.

"That I called things off with her for good," he told me. "Adrienne, I mean. We're not together anymore. I don't want anything to do with her."

I wondered how she had taken that. I doubted that she had been too delighted to find that out, that she had shot herself in the foot with not one but two powerful, rich men who could have made her life way easier than it needed to be. Some cruel part of me wished that I could have seen that unfold right in front of me, but honestly, I didn't give a fuck. There was some satisfaction in knowing that she hadn't gotten what she wanted, but not much. Because she didn't have a place in my head anymore.

"Good for you," I replied dryly. "I hope she doesn't manage to make you change your mind like she did all those other times."

Matt smirked, and quickly wiped it off his face. We weren't exactly in the place where we could joke about this as though nothing at all had happened yet. But he was still my business partner. There was nothing that I could do to change that, unless I wanted to admit to the whole world what he had been up to behind my back. I knew that if people got a sniff of instability in our business, they would descend on us to try to make the most of it, like the vultures they were. That was the last thing I needed right now.

"I should be out of town for the next couple of weeks," he finished up. "If you need me for anything…"

"I think I'll be just fine without you," I told him, my voice edged with a hardness that told him that I wasn't fucking around. He nodded, as though he knew it was what he deserved. Opening his mouth to say something else, he seemed to think better of it after a moment, and instead, turned to walk on out of my office and leave me in peace once more.

As soon as the door closed behind him, I reached under the table and grabbed my book once more. It was one of Alicia's. I still couldn't believe it had taken me as long as it had to get one of these things, and that she had been hiding such a deliciously dirty secret from me all this time. God, she was a fantastic writer. Or maybe it was just that I could imagine doing all of this to her, could imagine just what her reactions would have been and just how hot it would be to see her writhe underneath my touch.

I couldn't believe that the two of us had waited so long to finally get down to what we were doing right now. It was so much fun that I was having a hard time wrapping my head around it. None of that worry about being judged, about not being able to be honest about what we wanted. We knew each other well enough that there was no holding back, no bothering to get in the way of ourselves with nerves. We were just honest, and it made our actual encounters with each other just the *hottest* shit that I had ever experienced in my life.

We'd talked a little about what this was going to mean for us, as friends, but I knew that delving too deeply into that would just make a mess of the good thing that we had going on. Should I have been a little more careful with my feelings? Probably. But there was something about being with her that made me want to dive in head first, especially after the mess that my last relationship had ended up in.

Honestly, being with Alicia was the perfect palate-cleanser that I needed to get myself back on the proverbial dating horse. Adrienne had never been that wild in bed, and I had never felt the need to switch things up or try new stuff when I was with her – of course, now I knew that she had been getting it somewhere else, hence her lack of interest in me. But with Alicia, I could just throw myself at anything I thought sounded cool. Her books were giving me lots to work with, that was for sure, and I was taking every chance that I had, even at work, to read them and take in all the details of what she seemed to want.

I'd had no idea that my best friend had this much sheer kink inside of her. It turned me on, actually, just knowing that she had carved out these books about me – that so many women across the country had their hands down their panties at the thought of me doing all this stuff to them. Okay, so most of it I hadn't actually done before, but no point ruining the fantasy with something as banal as the truth, right?

I had never really considered that this was stuff that I could be into. Nobody had ever seen me this way, I supposed - in this dominant position, taking total control and command of everything and everyone around me. But I supposed that I was doing that, whether I recognized it or not – after all, I ran this company, and I pretty much had a hold over this whole office now that Matt had opted to go out of town for a while to make sure that I didn't eat him alive the first chance I got. Maybe I *was* good at this side of things; I had just never considered taking it a little further, into the bedroom.

I had always thought that I would feel silly doing something like that, acting like I was in total control of the woman who was with me, but honestly, those little experiments I had tried with Alicia, they had made me feel good. Just small things – like pinning her arms above her head, telling her when I wanted her to come, stuff like that – but they had been enough to send that shock of power through me. And it turned me on knowing that she was getting off on it just the same way I was. Honestly, there wasn't much that I wouldn't have done to please her if she had asked me to, and if she had called me up and asked me to turn up at her apartment with whips and chains and everything else, I would have done it in an instant.

Hmm. Now there was a thought. It could be fun to call her up right now, ask her to come down here. I had never had sex at the office, but now that Matt was going to make himself scarce for a while, it would have been rude not to take advantage of the extra space and time to do something fun, right? She worked from home, so it wasn't like there would be anything specific keeping her attention right now. Nothing that I couldn't distract her from, anyway...

The scene I had been on in her book was one that depicted this delicious blowjob, one where her leading man had taken total control and demanded all this attention for himself – even the thought of Alicia's mouth on my cock was enough to get me stirring beneath my pants, and I knew that I wasn't going to be able to restrain myself much longer.

I grabbed my phone, dialed her number, and reached between my legs and gripped my hardening erection. All she could say was no, right? Though I got the feeling that she wasn't going to pass up the chance to get her hands on me right now.

"Hello?" she greeted me after a couple of rings. I made sure that the door to my office was closed, and swiveled around in my seat just in case, to make sure that nobody would overhear me.

"I want you to come down to my office right now," I told her. "I have something for you."

She inhaled sharply on the other end of the line, and I could practically see the smile spreading over her face as she took in what I had just said to her.

"I'll be there in twenty," she replied, and she hung up. And, leaning back in my seat, I grinned and picked the book up once more. Damn, this thing was just *full* of bright ideas.

10

ALICIA

Trying to stem the little bubble of laughter that was threatening to rise up in my throat, I signed in at his desk downstairs, and then headed for the elevator so that I could go see Cameron once more.

I still couldn't quite believe that he had really called me up in the middle of the day to ask me to come by his office for – well, what for, I wasn't quite certain yet, but I got the feeling that I was going to enjoy the hell out of it. He had been reading my books lately, and I couldn't help but wonder if he had been inspired by a scene in my second novel, which just so happened to take place in an office not too far removed from this one.

But I was going to have to find some way to get my head around it sooner rather than later, because yes, this was really, truly, actually happening. The two of us had been officially hooking up since the week before last, and it had been so much fun that I had almost forgotten that we were meant to be friends first and lovers second. He really knew what he was doing when it came to being in bed with me, and I was already starting to get obsessed with the way he touched me, held me, fucked me. He could be gentle, but he could be a little rougher, sometimes, too, and I liked that more than I would have cared to admit.

Because that would have been coming clean about the fact that all these fantasies I had built around him had been within my reach all along. I had just been too scared to go out there and take what I knew to be mine. He was as amazing as I had imagined he would be, as I had always written he would be, and I knew that he was enjoying it just as much as I was. But I had held back all this time for fear that I would be let down, and that it would put a gun to the head of our friendship. Well, now, I knew that I had just been missing out on a good thing for no particular reason, and I had no intention at all of making that mistake again. Now that I had him, I wasn't about to let him go anywhere, that was for damn sure.

I nodded politely to the people in the elevator with me, and hoped that my hastily thrown-together outfit looked like it could pass for something professional; I'd been doing some edits in my pajamas when he had called me up, and I figured that I might as well play this game properly if I was going to play it at all. I didn't have a huge amount that could pass for professional, but I managed to dig out an old skirt-suit that I had worn to interviews when I had still been looking for a real job to supplement all that writing. I knew that it wasn't much, but nobody had done a double-take at me or anything, so I was pretty sure that I was sliding under the radar.

I felt a little giddy as I walked to the door, not quite able to believe that I was going to do this. But how could I say no? All this time, I had been writing about what these bold, adventurous women liked to get up to. Now that I had the chance to enjoy the same thing, there was no way in hell that I was going to skip out on the chance. It would have been honestly irresponsible for my career to even think about passing this up. Especially when I could be going down, instead...

I knocked on the door with his name embossed on the front and shot a look around to make sure that nobody was paying too much attention to me. Much to my relief, everyone looked as though they were caught up with their own busy days, and couldn't care less what I was doing heading to the boss' office. A moment later, the door opened, and I felt a hand on my wrist tugging me inside.

"You made it," Cameron remarked, as soon as he had the door shut behind us. I nodded and perched on the edge of his desk and gazed up at him, as though I had no idea at all what I might have been doing here.

"Yes, and I'd love it if you could let me know just *what* I made it for," I replied, but before I could come out with anything else too smart for my own good, he grasped my face in his hands, and kissed me.

I felt myself melt as soon as our lips met. How could I not? There was something so impossibly sweet about feeling him kiss me like this, even though I knew that it was the middle of the day inside his office, and that anyone could have walked in and caught the two of us together if we weren't more careful. I planted my hands on his chest and felt the beat of his heart beneath the pale blue shirt that he was wearing.

"I was reading your book," he murmured to me, pulling back. "I got to that part..."

"About the blowjob, in the office?" I replied, as I reached down between his legs. He was already hard as I skimmed my fingers over his erection, and he sucked in a sharp inhale at the feel of my touch. I grinned. Oh, it was just way too tempting to deny him right now, to tease him to see how he would react. But I hadn't come all the way down here not to get what I wanted. I wasn't going to back out now I was so damn close.

"The very same," he replied, and I guided him back towards his seat and pushed him down into it. He grinned as I sank down to the floor in front of him, shifting my skirt demurely, as though I wasn't getting down here to suck his beautiful cock.

"And you were hoping that we could re-enact that?" I asked, as I reached up to unbutton his pants. He nodded, reaching down to brush a strand of hair away from my face.

"I thought we might."

"Of course, sir," I replied playfully, but addressing him by that title made something inside of me start to heat up. I knew it was just a word, but it seemed to hold so much power, so much more than I had realized.

I stroked him a couple of times once I had him in my hand, admiring his full length – a solid seven inches, thick around the base, impressive against my small fingers. Flicking my gaze up to meet his, I leaned forward and, slowly, slowly, guiding him into my mouth.

"Fuck," he growled, and he reached down to grip hold of my shoulder, as though he was making sure that I didn't go anywhere at all. Not that I had any plans to. I swirled my tongue around his tip and then took him deeper, letting him slide as far into me as I could without hitting the back of my throat. I could already taste the ooze of his salty precum on my tongue, and I took my time to seal my lips around him and slide all the way up and off, getting him good and wet with my saliva as I did so.

And it was the strangest thing – as I did that to him, for him, I found myself sinking into the role that I had made for myself within my books. I took my time, lavishing his cock with attention – flicking my tongue just against the tip a couple of times, and then swallowing as much as I could of him whole, taking my time and lapping all the way from the head to the base and back again, and then sliding my mouth up and down at a greater pace than before. I had always been a little nervous about giving head myself, but now, I felt as though I had been emboldened by the spirit of the woman that

I had written for so long. And she knew *what the hell* she was doing.

"You look so good like that," he told me, and I flicked my eyes up to meet his again. God, there was something so hot about seeing the way he watched me when I was blowing him, as though there was nothing else in the world that he would rather have been looking at in that moment. I wrapped my fingers around him again, stroked him a couple of times, trailed my tongue around my lips.

"Like what?" I asked him. I needed to hear him say it. I wasn't sure why, but I needed that much.

"With my cock in your mouth," he told me, and with that, I took him once more. Hearing him talk to me like that turned me on in ways that I didn't think were possible until this little affair of ours had started for real.

I pushed his cock back for a moment so that I could press my mouth to his balls, taking them in between my lips one at a time – they were heavy and smooth and a little addictive, or at least the way he reacted when I was sucking on them was. I continued to stroke him as I licked on the wrinkled skin, enjoying the tension I could already feel spreading through his thighs. He was getting close. How long had he been imagining me like this, down between his legs, worshipping his cock like it was the most perfect thing that I had ever seen in my entire life before?

Once he seemed satisfied with my ball-sucking, he reached down and pulled my head back onto his dick. The closer he got to the edge, the more he seemed to take control. I liked that, liked pushing him as far as he would go just to see when he would tip past the point of no return. I let him slide himself all the way up to the hilt, his cock buried in my throat; I nearly gagged on it, but I managed to hold it inside of me, and I looked up at him again, needing the validation of his arousal to get me where I needed to go. His eyes were dark and filled with lust that

I knew was for me and me alone, and I could feel the wetness beginning to leak between my thighs, more than I could take. I moved my hand between my legs, keen for any relief that I could find, any at all.

He began to push his hips back up to meet me, pressing his cock deeper into my mouth, and I knew that he was getting close. I didn't take my eyes from his as I allowed him to use my face however he wanted. He could have asked me to do anything for him in that moment, and I would have been more than willing to just let him take control of my body and do whatever he wanted with me, to me.

Suddenly, I felt his cock twitch in my mouth, and he let out a groan as he filled my mouth with his sperm. I could taste his salty-sweetness, and I let out a moan as I felt the satisfaction of it course through my body. I was enough. I could give him everything he needed. I closed my eyes, savored the moment, allowed myself to get lost in it...

Right up until the moment, of course, the door opened behind us. And I realized that we were totally and utterly busted.

11

CAMERON

"You have to be fucking kidding me."

As soon as Matt walked into my office, I knew that I had sincerely and truly fucked up.

Matt had returned from his trip early, after he'd heard what had happened between Alicia and me in this very office. I still couldn't believe that the two of us had gotten caught – and that everyone in this damn office knew that I was hardly the cool, calm, collected guy I'd always sold myself as around here.

I could still remember the situation as it had unfolded, as it was burned into my memory so vividly that I feared I would never forget the way that it felt. The door had sprung open, to reveal my secretary, Talia, standing there in the doorway. And there was no way that I could pretend that what was happening wasn't going down right now. I tried to pull Alicia to her feet before the two of us got caught, but it was way too late.

She had seen everything. And, though she tried to back out of there as quickly as she could, she couldn't hide the fact that she had taken in every detail of what we had just been caught doing, and that there was no way she was going to be able to keep her mouth shut about it. Talia was the biggest gossip in this entire fucking place, and sure enough, it didn't take long until the news had spread back to Matt and he had returned to the office to confront me once more.

"You didn't really do it, did you?" he asked, as he stood there over my desk, glaring down at me like he couldn't believe he was actually having to have this conversation with me. Shit, it wasn't as though I had been looking forward to it, either.

"I mean, I know you, man," he continued. "You're not that guy. Talia's just talking shit, isn't she? Like, someone bent down to grab a pencil and then she walked in and she saw something that looked worse than it was..."

"No, it happened," I replied, bluntly. There was no point in hiding what had happened between us; Matt knew me well enough to see through me when I was lying, and besides, it wasn't like my denying it could undo the fact that pretty much everyone in this office believed it as fact by now. Unless I was going to go around and deny it to everyone in person, the news was out there, and there was nothing that I could do to reel it back in now that it had gotten away from me.

"Shit," Matt muttered, and he closed the door behind him so that nobody else could hear what we were talking about.

"We need to do some serious damage control," he told me, pacing back and forth at once, fingers on his temples, as though he was trying to rub out a decent idea. There was some part of me that wanted to throw back in his face just what he had done to me in the recent past, but I knew that wasn't going to help anything. A CEO getting blown in his office was actually relevant to the work that we were doing here, and there was no way I was going to be able to slide that under the radar. People would hear about it, and it wouldn't take long until I had managed to earn myself a reputation around here. Which was the last thing I needed. When shit like that happened, it came before business, and we needed to shut it off before it overtook the press around any new deals we had going on.

"And how are we going to do that?" I asked. I didn't exactly want him to be here, not really, but I figured I didn't have much of a choice right now. I mean, if I were to kick him out and tell him not to come back, that would be as good as admitting to what had happened with him and Adrienne, and the last thing we needed was more scandal right now. Though I could have done without him right now, I knew there was nobody else who could handle this the way that he could.

"First, you need to make sure that this girl never comes back here," he told me. "Who is she, by the way? Anyone I need to know about?"

"You know her," I admitted. "It's Alicia. My old roommate, you remember?"

He came to a standstill and paused for a moment to stare at me. It was like all the blood from his face had just drained out all at once. I knew that this was bad, somehow, in ways that I hadn't yet figured out.

"Seriously?" he replied, and I nodded.

"Why? It's not that big a deal," I fired back, more defensive than I had to be.

"Were you with her when you and Adrienne were together?" he asked me, and I shook my head at once.

"I'm not a cheat," I replied, a little sharper than I intended. I knew that shooting bullets at him wasn't going to help anything, but I was still pissed that I was in this situation right now. I couldn't believe I had been so stupid. I wanted to figure myself out, but I knew I needed Matt to take the edge off this before it got out of control.

"Yeah, sure," he replied. "That's not my main concern right now. Just make sure she doesn't come back to the office, okay? And no other women in here, either. We don't want this breaking out into some sort of pandemic of you getting caught doing shit that you shouldn't. You might have split with Adrienne, but we're trying to maintain the image of you as an actually decent guy, okay?"

"Okay," I agreed. "So what else can I do?"

"Make sure you don't do anything that's going to cause a stir around here," he told me firmly. "You need to keep your head down and make sure that nobody has any reason to even look at you sideways. You got that?"

"I've got that," I replied, and I felt a swell of dread in my chest. This was exactly the shit that I didn't want to get caught up in. I knew this was my fault, but that didn't make it any easier to handle. I had always prided myself on being sensible, on being the one who knew how to live his life without causing a stir. And yet, I had thought that calling up my friend-with-benefits to come down to my office and hook up was okay. All because I had been reading those books she had written, and I had decided I was just as bold and forward and powerful as the man she had based on me.

Well, those books were fiction, and that man didn't have to worry about getting caught in the act. He didn't have to think about making a mess of his office by playing too big for his boots. And in future, I was going to remember that.

"I need to go downstairs, check if anyone's spoken to people outside of the office about this," Matt told me, rubbing his hand over his face as though this was the very last thing he wanted to have to think about. "Try not to get caught up in the middle of any scandals, okay?"

"Okay," I muttered, and with that, he stalked out of the office and closed the door tight behind him. I knew he had every right to be as mad with me as he was, but there was still some stubborn part of me that knew I didn't want to let him off the hook for Adrienne that easily. Still, if he could contain this, I guessed I would have to start letting off the heat a little.

Shit. I was so fucking angry with myself. I always turned it in on myself when shit like this happened, and I knew I had only myself to blame for the mess I was currently sitting in. I had let myself get carried away, and I needed to get myself in hand and remind myself of what actually mattered. Which was focusing on my job and getting my life back together again after my fiancée had made a mess of it for me.

What I had been doing with Alicia, it was a mistake. I hated to admit it, but I could see that now. I loved her, of course I did, but she was my friend – even though the sex was awesome, I knew that we couldn't keep going with this. It was just too dangerous. Being together in that way, it was going to make our friendship harder to maintain, especially if I was going to continue to insist on calling her into the office to do crazy shit when I should have been working.

None of this mess would have happened if I hadn't gone around to her apartment after I had been on that date. I could have called her on the use of my life in her books, it could have been a joke between us – there were so many ways that I could have shared little details of everything that was happening with me without sleeping with her, weren't there? But I had looked at those stories, and I had known that I needed more.

Well, I wasn't going to make that mistake again. Not a chance in hell. I was going to call things off with her and put it down to a mistake that the two of us could laugh about in a few days' time. Okay, maybe a few months. If we could ever get back to where we had been at all…

I pulled my phone out of my pocket and shot her a text, telling Alicia that we needed to talk, and sooner rather than later. I hadn't spoken to her since the two of us had been caught in the office, and I had no idea how she felt about all of it. Maybe she was as humiliated as I was, maybe she was worried that she had caused more trouble than she could handle – maybe she had enjoyed some part of getting caught in the act, even though it had been a total mess. I had no idea. Because this version of Alicia was one that I didn't know. I might have called her my best friend, but everything that had happened between us had underlined the fact that I really didn't have a clue who she was or what I could expect from her.

And maybe that was the way it should have stayed. I liked being with her, but I didn't want to lose my best friend to the fling that we were having here. I was never going to be that guy. She was more important to me than that, and there was no way that I was going to forget it. Sex was one thing, but the kindness she had showed me, the sweetness that she had given me, the support that we'd had for one another, that was more important than anything physical.

I leaned back in my seat and let out a long sigh. Okay, so I was ready to put this all behind me. I just had to hope that this went as smoothly as it could, and that she didn't get hurt in the process. The last few weeks had been a total mess, but I was ready to get back to reality, and put all of that behind me. Life went on. And I was more than ready to move the hell on from this entire mess once and for all.

12

ALICIA

I stepped back inside my apartment, pushed the door closed behind me, and let out a little groan as soon as I heard it click into the lock.

I couldn't believe it. *I couldn't believe it.* When things had been going so well, too – okay, so there had been that little blip in the proceedings with being caught in the office, but it wasn't anything that we wouldn't have been able to move past given a little time. Yet Cameron had called it all off, once and for all. And I could hardly believe how much it hurt now that it was over.

"It's just not a good idea right now," Cameron had told me over coffee, at the same place where we had agreed to start all of this so recently. How could it be done already? We had only just gotten started. There was so much for us left to learn about one another, and I couldn't believe that he didn't want to explore it the same way that I did.

"You know that I still want to be your friend, but I'm worried that all of this is going to get in the way of that," he continued, as I sat there, staring into my coffee and feeling like I had been kicked in the guts. Okay, so being caught in the act had hardly been what I was hoping for, but shit happened, right? He had been the one to call me up and ask me to come around there in the first place, and he must have known that there were risks to that. I had thought he realized all of that, but it seemed like all of this was pretty new to him – that he was taking some time to wrap his head around what this meant, what being involved in something hot and heavy and hungry could do to you.

"I get it," I replied, but the words had sounded hollow when they came out of my mouth. I wanted to respect his wishes, and I would never have pushed him to do something that he didn't want to do. But I would have been lying if I'd said that there wasn't a part of me that was already mourning the loss of what we had experienced together. After all that time writing those stories, I had really found myself caught up in an affair with the very man that I had been telling tales about all that time. I couldn't think of anything better. And now, it had been taken away from me before I'd really had a chance to explore it, and I didn't know how I was meant to cope with that.

"So, back to normal?" he asked, as he extended his hand towards me. I looked down at it. Were we there again? Handshakes? Pretending that none of it had ever happened?

"Back to normal," I replied. Because I knew that telling him the truth was going to lose me any chance to be around him at all.

"But if you need any details for the books, you can ask away," he offered, as we shook hands. I clamped my hand back on my lap, looking down at the one that had touched him, wondering if it would be the last chance that I ever got to do that the way I wanted.

"Yeah, good to know," I replied, and I tried to sound bright and light around the edges. I knew that I needed to make him believe that I had just brushed this off, even if I hadn't.

"It's just about work," he went on, and it seemed as though

he was trying to make as many excuses as he could, to bolster himself against the thought of this ever happening again.

"I can't let anything like that get in the way of the office," he continued. I looked up at him, wondering if I should say it out loud.

"You know, we could...we don't have to..." I replied, and he cocked his head at me. And, as I looked at him, this man who just so happened to be the manifestation of so many of my fantasies, I closed my mouth again. I couldn't ask him to be that for me. It wasn't fair. He hadn't asked for me to write those books about him, to create some version of him that I adored so completely that the thought of letting go of him was more than I could bear. And I had to keep reminding myself that the stories I had written, they were nothing more than that – stories. Not reality. Nothing that reflected the truth.

Because the truth of being with him had been so much better than anything I ever could have come up with.

"What?" he prompted me, and I shook my head and looked away from him.

"Nothing," I muttered, hoping that I could make him believe me right now. I felt as though the ground had been tipped out from underneath me, like I was sliding off the edge and needed to find something to hang on to before I plunged over the edge.

"I should never have let this happen in the first place," he told me, and each word out of his mouth was like a strike to my heart. Did he really feel that badly about it? I felt like what we'd had, it had been amazing, but he was talking about it as though it was already distant history and he could see it with the full clarity of retrospection.

"You're my friend, and you know that I love you as that," he continued. "I don't want anything to get in the way of that, and I know that if we carry on with this, that's going to happen."

I chewed my lip. Okay, so I didn't exactly disagree with him there. I could already feel myself falling for him, just a little – I knew him so well, and all that it had taken was an acceptance of the chemistry that we had to tip over into the real romance that I didn't even know I had been craving for so long. But I was okay with that. Maybe I even wanted that. I wrote so much about people falling into these crazy, passionate relationships, and all this time I had thought that they were nothing more than fiction, but now, looking at this man sitting opposite me, I could have believed that they existed right here in the real world.

"Yeah, I suppose so," I muttered, and I looked away from him again. Looking right at him, when he was telling me all of this – it was too painful for me to bear right now. I couldn't believe how deep the pit in my stomach felt right now. We had only been doing this a couple of weeks. How could I already feel this way about him?

"I guess I should get going," I told him, and I chugged the last of my too-hot coffee and hoped that I wasn't making my discomfort too obvious.

"You don't want something to eat?" he asked, and I shook my head. I couldn't have eaten anything right now – my stomach was in knots, and I knew that my appetite wasn't going to come back for days. I felt so foolish. So stupid for thinking that I could actually make this work, that it wasn't going to fall apart at the seams. That I wasn't going to get feelings for this man.

"No, I'm good," I replied, and I grabbed my coat and tossed it over my shoulders. I didn't want to be here a moment longer. The further I could get from him, the better – the further I could get from him, the easier it would have been to pretend that none of this had happened in the first place.

I made my way out of the coffee shop and headed straight back to my apartment as soon as I could get there. When the door shut behind me, I felt tears prick my eyes. How could I already feel this way about him? Why was it that I felt as though

I had just been through a breakup? It wasn't like I was never going to get to see him again. We were still friends. We just wouldn't be hooking up anymore, because we had gone a little too far too fast and now we needed to get ourselves back to reality once more.

I had split up with Jerry recently, and it hadn't felt anything like this. It had just been like cutting someone loose, someone who had been dragging me backwards anyway. But this? No, this was something far heavier than that, something that I hadn't been ready for.

And there was only one thing that I did when I felt this way, when there were emotions in my guts that I couldn't figure out, and that was to write. I made my way over to the computer and booted it up, staring at my reflection in the blank screen for the seconds before it flicked on in front of me. I looked drawn and tired, as though I hadn't slept for days. Shit, that conversation had really taken it out of me. And now, I had to deal with what came next.

As soon as the computer was switched on, I opened up a new document and started to write. I didn't know what I was going to use this for, but I needed to get these words out of me once and for all, before they got stuck just rolling around and around my head with no way to get out.

The words came pouring out of me, and I found myself feeling as though there was a weight lifting from my shoulders. And I found that they were taking the form of the stories that I had always told. I might have just finished the last part, but maybe this could be the next one. Maybe Andrew and Lana could really go through something, once and for all, maybe they could break up and I could work out a way to make the audience believe that it was possible. Because all this time, I had let them just be in love, instead of stirring up trouble. But the more time that passed, the more that I could see that it just wasn't realistic for them to live that way. People didn't always stay together. No matter how perfect they might have seemed for one another, sometimes things just didn't work out, and I understood that better than ever now.

I wasn't sure how long I sat there, just writing, but by the time that I was done, the sun had started to set outside once more, and I felt like I just wanted to curl up in bed with the covers over my head and pretend that the world outside didn't exist. I knew that I would have to figure this out one way or another – that just pouring all of this into my stories wouldn't actually exorcise it from me properly – but for now, at least, it was enough to get it out of my head.

I had written a few thousand words by the time I sat back from the computer. I still had no appetite, but I knew that I needed to eat something before I starved to death right there in my apartment. Maybe I should have taken Cameron up on his offer of food back at the coffee shop – but that would have meant spending even more time with him. And I knew that another minute in his presence would have been too much for me to handle. I was back by myself once more, and maybe I would be better off for it. Maybe.

13

CAMERON

I woke up to the sound of a banging on my door, and I lifted my head from the pillow and squinted my eyes against the morning light. What the hell was happening? Was the apartment building on fire?

I peeled myself out of bed, rubbing my hands over my face and reaching for a shirt to throw on over my bare chest; I had no idea who this was, and the last thing I needed right now was to accidentally expose myself to whoever wanted to see me so urgently.

"Coming, coming," I muttered, as I made my way over to the door. I didn't know who it could be. It wasn't like there were many people who knew where I was staying these days, not since I had moved out of the place I had lived in with Adrienne. I had specifically made a point of keeping all of that under wraps, wanting a new start, but it looked like someone had managed to track me down.

And, when I opened the door, my heart sank as I saw who was waiting for me on the other side.

"Adrienne," I groaned when I saw her, still poised with a lifted fist to continue her battery against my door.

"What the hell are you doing here?" I demanded. It was too early for this shit, that was for sure, but I got the feeling that she didn't care.

"I heard about what happened at your office," she replied, storming past me without even waiting for an invitation. I had seen her on this warpath a few times before, and I knew that there was no point trying to intervene or get in the way of whatever justified rage that she was on for the time being.

"What are you talking about?" I asked her, trying to sound as neutral as possible. Matt must have passed it along to her. He'd said that they weren't in touch anymore, but maybe he felt justified in sharing what had happened given that I had made my own indiscretion in his eyes.

"You and that Alicia bitch," she spat at me. And I bristled angrily at the sound of her using that word. We might not have been involved anymore, but that didn't mean Alicia wasn't my friend anymore, and there was no way I was going to let Adrienne speak about her that way.

"Don't call her that," I shot back, a warning tone to my voice. She narrowed her eyes at me and planted her hands on her hips.

"So, you got so up in arms about me seeing Matt," she snapped at me. "But all this time, you were seeing her behind my back?"

"What are you talking about?" I demanded, and she shook her head, a callous smile spreading across her face as though she had been saving this all up to unleash on me at once.

"I looked over those silly books that she writes," she explained. "And they're all about you. Matt told me what you guys were caught getting up to in your office; that's right out of one of her books. So, how long has it been going on, then? How long have you been seeing her?"

"You're talking shit," I told her bluntly. "We weren't together

– we haven't been together. We've just been friends this whole time."

"Oh, yeah, sure, very friendly to invite her over to your office and have her blow you," she shot back angrily. "What did you tell me? You asked if I was just re-inflating him, right? What, was it the same for you, or is it different when you're the one in the middle of it?"

"You don't know what you're talking about," I snarled at her. I knew that I shouldn't have allowed her to get under my skin like this, but I was still raw from having to call things off with Alicia the day before, and there was no way that I was going to let Adrienne come and stir shit up when there was no shit at all to stir.

"Oh, I think I do," she fired back. "Come on, don't act like I'm an idiot. I can tell she was writing about you that whole time. And what? You were sleeping with her on the side? When you were dating me? Did you tell yourself that it was just research so it didn't count?"

"You need to get out of here," I warned her. I still didn't even know how she had found my house in the first place, but I was going to make sure that she never came back.

"You need to tell me the truth," she told me hotly, turning to face me and planting her hands on her hips. She was angry, I could tell that, so angry that she wasn't going to let me tell her what was really going on here. I hated this. I wished I could have just reached out to her and told her that she was crazy, that she needed to listen to the words coming out of her mouth, to know if she really believed anything she was saying right now. She might have been cheating on me when we had been together, but I had been honest with her, and she must have known that I didn't have it in me to treat her that way.

"I am telling you the truth," I told her, teeth gritted. I felt like I was going to flip a table if she didn't get out of here soon. I needed my space to work out how I felt about this whole mess with Alicia, and having my bullshit, cheating ex turn up on my doorstep to accuse me of stuff that I had never done in the first place wasn't making that easy, to be sure.

"Come on, just be honest with me," she goaded me again, and I knew she was trying to push my buttons now. I wasn't going to let her do this to me. I wasn't going to let her win.

"I've been honest with you from the start," I shot back at her. "I'm not the one who was cheating on you all the way through our relationship, remember?"

"Oh, don't play all high and mighty with me now," she snapped, shaking her head. "I've read those books. Shit, I only skimmed them, and there was enough in there to prove that the two of you were sleeping together for pretty much the whole time we were together!"

"And what does it matter if we were?" I demanded, feeling defeated all of a sudden. "You cheated on me, remember? You can't exactly claim the moral high ground here."

She crossed her arms over her chest and looked at me, and I could tell that she had some serious plan in the works right now. Shit. This was the last thing I needed. More drama than I knew what to do with. This was what happened when I dived into what I really wanted – more mess than I knew what to do with landed right on my lap where I couldn't do anything about it.

"I want you to support me," she replied, as though it should have been obvious. My jaw dropped.

"I'm sorry, what did you just say?" I replied.

"I want you to support me," she repeated again. "I mean, we were meant to be married, right? It's just alimony, really."

"Yeah, that you forfeited as soon as you got involved with my business partner," I pointed out, and she shook her head and took a step towards me.

"That's not how it works," she replied, and she lowered her voice, knowing that she had all the power in this situation.

"Because Matt was meant to take care of me after you were out of the picture," she explained. "And he's crapped out on that out of some misguided loyalty to you, no doubt. Well, I'm not going to live the rest of my life without anyone to take care of me, especially since I was being cheated on the whole time that we were together."

"I'm not paying you a fucking cent," I warned her, and a smile licked up her lips. She didn't look like she gave much of a damn.

"I don't think you have much of a choice," she replied. "Either you start paying me, or I'm going to make sure that everyone knows just what you've been getting up to with Alicia. And that you're the basis for those books that she's been writing all this time."

I stared at her. There was no way she would hit that button, was there? She might have been a callous bitch, but that would have been a lot even for her. More than I thought she was capable of. But the way she was looking at me, I knew she was just daring me to argue with her, to make a scene and push back. Because she had nothing left to lose, and that was a dangerous place for her to be in right now.

"So, I'll leave it up to you," she told me, as though she had laid out something totally reasonable to me. I couldn't fucking believe this. I couldn't *believe* it. All this mess, all this chaos, all this because I hadn't been able to keep my dick in my pants when I had been at work.

"But I figured that I would at least give you the chance to make sure that your reputation stays clean before I tell everyone I can find about your little affair with that smut writer," she finished up. Running her fingers through her hair, she let out a long breath, and smiled. She seemed almost serene, even though the smile didn't come close to reaching her eyes.

"You're crazy," I told her, but she just shrugged. It didn't seem to bother her what I called her, and that meant that she believed that she had nothing to fear. She had all the power. And she knew it.

"I might be, but it's up to you to figure out what you want to do with it," she replied. And with that, she turned on the spot, and headed to the door. She paused for a moment in the frame, looking over her shoulder at me to make sure that I had understood just what she was laying out for me here.

"So, either I have a payment in my account by the end of the week," she announced. "Say, a thousand dollars? Or you're going to find yourself at the center of an even *bigger* scandal than you're already dealing with right now."

Seemingly satisfied, she turned on her heel and walked out of the apartment, making sure to slam the door behind her. The shock of the sound made me jump and, a moment later, the deafening silence in the apartment was more than I could bear.

What the fuck was I going to do now? I didn't want to spend the rest of my life looking after that bitch, but at the same time – if it came out that I was the one that all those stories had been based on, then I would have a serious problem. We were a family-friendly business, and if people caught wind of the fact that I had been involved in something like that, even if it had been without my knowledge – shit, there would be hell to pay. I thought I'd had a problem before, but that was nothing compared to the issue that was arising now that Adrienne had decided to inject herself back into the picture.

I slumped down into the couch, hoping it would swallow me up. And as I sat there, I tried to come up with something that could get this whole situation under control.

14

ALICIA

"Cameron?"

I was sure when I saw him standing outside my apartment that I had just invented him in my head – that he was a mirage meant to fill in the gaps of how much I wanted to see him again. But now, he was here, he was real, and he looked as though he had been run down by a fucking train.

"Alicia," he murmured to me in greeting, and he pulled me into a tight hug. I grasped hold of him tight and closed my eyes, wondering what the hell had brought him here, but not willing to question it too much, not when it felt so damn good to be close to him like this again.

"What are you doing here?" I asked him. He nodded to my door.

"Do you mind if we talk about it inside?" he asked, and I glanced over my shoulder, wondering what was so serious that he needed the privacy of my home to talk about it.

"Sure, of course," I promised him, and I opened it up and the two of us headed upstairs and back to my apartment.

I couldn't help but think, of course, about the fact that the last time he had been here was the first time that I had really seen him for what he was. When he had come right from that date to my apartment, to ask what the hell I had been doing with the version of him that I had put into my stories. It had started there, this mess that was going on inside my head right now, the memory of everything that we had done together. I wasn't sure if I wanted to rewind time to erase it – or just so I got a chance to relive it again.

"What's going on?" I asked him, as I headed into the kitchen to make us both a coffee. I had been heading out to get myself some breakfast, but seeing him again had made my stomach loop-the-loop so much that I couldn't think of consuming much more than caffeine for the time being.

"I...there's something happening," he confessed. "And it involves you, so I thought that you would want to hear about it."

"What do you mean?" I asked, feeling a creeping dread rush up the back of my neck. I couldn't handle anything else right now. But still, anything that brought the two of us together had to be a good thing, didn't it? Maybe I didn't mind as much as I felt like I did.

"Adrienne came to my apartment this morning," he confessed. "She heard about what happened between us from Matt; seems like the two of them are still in touch."

"And?" I prompted him. "Things are over with you guys, right? So it's not a big deal?"

"Yeah, that's what I would have thought," he replied, shaking his head. "But she told me that she'd read some of your books. She put the pieces together, it seems – she knows that I'm the one you based this character on. And she thinks that I was cheating on her with you the whole time that we were together."

"That's crazy," I protested. "We were just friends, nothing ever happened..."

"Trust me, I know that," he replied with a sigh. "But she's convinced. And she wants me to...well, she's asked me to support her, or else she's going to tell anyone who'll listen that I'm the one in those stories."

"Holy shit," I gasped. I couldn't believe it. One, that Adrienne had actually had the guile to put all those pieces together and figure out that I had been the one behind all of it. And two – that I had been the cause of such a major source of stress in his life.

"She's asking you to support her?" I pressed, shaking my head. "She can't make you do that, can she?"

"She can't make me," he replied. "But she's saying it's like alimony – it's just what I owe her after the breakup. She thinks I cheated, and she thinks this is what she's owed."

"That's the craziest thing I've ever heard in my life," I replied, staring down at the coffee that I had made myself. I couldn't have written anything more outrageous than this.

"Yeah, tell me about it," he sighed. "But I don't see how I can get out of this. I don't want her to tell anyone – if she could put the pieces together, and that girl I was on the date with could, then there must be enough in those books that other people can figure it out, too. And if it gets out that I'm anywhere near those stories..."

He shook his head and lowered his gaze to the ground below. I felt a flood of guilt. I had been the one to do this – even if I hadn't known that the character was really based on him until just recently, I had still been the one to put him in this position. I had made this mess. And I knew there was nothing I could do to make it better.

"I'm so sorry," I blurted out. "I can't...I should never..."

"You have nothing to be sorry for," he told me firmly. "This is Adrienne's doing, not yours. You're not the one who tried to turn this into a problem."

"Yeah, but if I had never written those books," I pointed out. "If I had never put that stuff out there, then..."

"Then we would never have had a chance to be together the

way we were," he replied, and there was a soft smile on his face that made my heart feel warm. I knew that it was dangerous, to let that sweetness spread through me, but when he looked at me like that it was impossible to deny my feelings for him.

"I guess," I agreed, and I swiftly drew my gaze away from him. "Why are you here? If there's nothing I can do to help?"

"Because I needed to tell you that this was coming," he replied simply. "I thought it was only fair. These are your books, after all, your stories."

"Thank you," I murmured, and I looked up at him. And, with a long inhale, he filled the silence between us. I knew there was something that he wanted to say to me, but I had no idea what it was. I didn't know if I was ready to hear it, but I sure as hell wasn't going to pull back now that we were so close.

"There's something else, too," he admitted. "I came here because I realized – well, I realized that I didn't want to do this without you."

"What do you mean?" I breathed, a swell of hope filling my chest like a warm bubble. Maybe, just maybe...

"I mean, I know that I'm going to have to go through this no matter what," he confessed, a small smile spreading over his lips.

"The worst thing that could happen, well, it's right in the process of happening right now," he went on. "And I'm not willing to give up on you in the process of this. I want to be with you, Alicia, I really do. And I don't want to let anything get in the way of that."

"You mean it?" I replied, feeling a little stupid, but needing to know one way or another that this was for real and not some twisted joke at my expense. The way he was looking at me, it was more than I could handle all at once, and I had no clue what to do with the flood of emotion that was coursing through me.

"I mean it," he told me. "The only reason I wanted to stop

was because I thought I could avert a disaster. But now that's happening – well, I don't see any good reason why I should pretend that I don't enjoy what we have together."

I felt a smile spread across my face, impossible to deny, impossible to hide. I didn't want to hide from him anymore. I had managed to lie to myself and to him yesterday, but I didn't know how I was meant to keep doing that when my heart felt like it beat to the sound of his name inside my chest.

"I want that too," I blurted out. "And I'm sorry, I'm sorry I caused so much of a mess for you – if I could change it, I would, but I want to be with you, Cameron. I like being with you. I know that we're friends and everything, and I don't want to lose that, but I don't think that we – I mean, I think this could be something more than that. Something better than that."

"I think so too," he agreed. And, slowly, he lifted his hand and placed it on my cheek. His touch was enough to send a shock of need through me, and I wondered, for the briefest moment, how I had ever thought that I would be able to get by as just his friend. Now that I had tasted what we had, I would never be able to go back to what we'd been before.

He leaned forward and pressed his forehead against mine. The warmth of his skin so close to my own made my body feel like it was lighting up with want. Did he feel the same thing? I gazed into his eyes and tried to search them for some sort of answer, but I had no idea how to read that in him yet. I was still learning him in this way, because he had been my friend for so long that I had to figure out how we functioned now that we had moved beyond that.

He touched his finger to my chin, and tilted my mouth up to meet his; as soon as our lips found each other's, I felt as though I had let out a sigh of relief that I hadn't even known that I had been holding all this time. It was a soft kiss, the kind of kiss that made my heart feel like it was going to burst out of my chest, but then it deepened, his tongue moving against mine so we could taste one another. I knew I had been the cause of a lot of stress in his life lately, but maybe I could make up for all of that. I could find some way to fix it and to make sure it was all worthwhile. At least, for now.

He guided me back on to the couch, moving on top of me so I could feel the full weight of his body on me. I wrapped my arms around him and wondered if this was some sort of fantasy, some sort of dream – maybe that feeling of all of this being a mirage when I had seen him outside was accurate, and none of this could actually be real. But as he smoothed my hair back from my head, I knew that I couldn't have come up with anything as detailed as this, even on my most creative days. He was more than I could have invented, and I wanted to keep this off the page for now, just for us.

"I can't believe I ever thought about letting you go," he murmured into my ear, and his voice was overheated and lusty and it made me feel like I was sinking into his body completely. As though there was no space between us anymore, not that I wanted there to be.

"Me neither," I replied, and I turned my head and kissed him again, harder this time, more passionately. To let him know that I wasn't going to let him make the same mistake, not ever again.

15

CAMERON

I pushed her legs apart and pushed my hips against hers; I couldn't believe that I had thought for a moment I could go without her, because it was so obvious to me now that there was no way in hell I would be able to survive without her at my side.

She moaned as she kissed me, her tongue in my mouth, and I reached to push open the sweater she had been wearing when I had turned up outside her house. She was all wrapped up against the weather, but in here, it was hot as hell and I wanted her naked.

I kissed down her throat as I undressed her quickly, moving my hands across her body hungrily as I stripped her down; my mouth continued downward as I brushed my lips over her clavicle, the curve of her breast, and then drew her nipple into my mouth, baring my teeth slightly and making her jump with the shock of it. I pressed down on her arms, keeping her in place, letting her know that there was no way that I was going to let her go anywhere right now.

"Fuck, you taste so good," I breathed to her, tracing my tongue over her swollen nipple, watching as it hardened under my touch. She flexed her hands beneath mine and looked down at me to watch as I lavished her with all the attention I knew she so keenly deserved.

"I missed this," she replied, and I grinned up at her.

"I've only been away a couple of days," I pointed out, and she grinned and wriggled beneath me.

"Yeah, well, that's just how good we are together," she replied, and I dove into her breasts once more, kissing and licking and squeezing at them so I could watch the way she reacted to every one of my touches.

And soon, I was traveling down – down, further and further, brushing my lips over the spot just below her belly and listening to the little moan of pleasure she let out in response. I knew she wanted this. I knew she meant it when she said she had missed it. And I intended to prove to her just how much I meant it, too.

Moving further, I unbuttoned her pants and pulled off her jeans. She had the most gorgeous legs I had ever seen, long and shapely, her thighs thick and enticing; I couldn't help but grip hold of them for a moment, squeeze to the shape of her, listen to the way she moaned again in response. I helped her kick off her pants, and then leaned down to plant a kiss against her panties.

"Fuck," she gasped, and she pulled a hand free and pushed her fingers through my hair, like she was making sure I didn't go anywhere right now. I slid my hands beneath her thighs and took hold of her panties, tugging them down over her hips and stripping her to total nakedness.

I let out a groan of pleasure as I slowly lowered my mouth back down to her slit; God, she tasted so good, her pussy already good and wet and ready for me as I stirred my tongue over her for the first time. She let out a helpless moan, her hands meshing in my hair to hold me in place, as though I had any intention at all of being anywhere else right now. I loved this. I was obsessed with her body, with the way it responded to me, and I knew that nothing was going to change that as long as she would let me pleasure her this way.

Slowly, I traced my tongue up to find her clit, swirling it around her engorged nub a couple of times before I sealed my lips to her and began to apply a gentle pressure. She gasped and pushed her hips back to meet me, grinding me hungrily against her pussy, and I gripped hold of her thighs and kept her in place and continued with the steady pressure of my lips and my tongue.

"Fuck, that feels so good," she gasped lustily. I pulled back for a moment, hovering my mouth over her for an instant, just to see the way she would react to me right now. She reached down and pushed me back against her pussy, and I took that as all the encouragement I needed to give her everything I wanted to.

I buried my face against her pussy, letting her grind herself back against me as I lavished her with attention – my tongue in circles around her clit, my fingers pressing against the entrance to her slit, teasing her with just an inch of penetration before pulling back once more. I wanted this to last as long as I could let it. I wanted to see how far I could push her before she would give and break and beg me for more.

"Oh my God," she groaned, and she was soon pushing her hips back on my mouth, her body moving as though it was possessed by something that had never moved inside of her before. I flicked my gaze up to watch her as she got closer, the tension that took over her jaw, the way her whole system seemed to be trembling as she edged closer and closer to the edge.

"Are you going to come?" I asked her, pulling back for just a moment, long enough for her to let out this helpless half-cry in response to the sudden cessation of sensation.

"Yes, yes," she gasped, and she arched her back from the couch and I took the signal as all the invitation I needed. I buried my face against her pussy and lapped at her clit, and a moment later, I felt her whole body start as the orgasm rocked through her. She didn't make a sound, but she didn't need to – the contraction of her muscles, the tension of her thighs around my head, that told me everything I needed to know. I didn't move my mouth, kept pleasuring her as she came, until she pushed me back and gasped for air.

I dove on top of her and kissed her again, letting her taste her wetness on my lips; she wrapped her legs around me and pushed her hips back towards me, letting out these pathetic little mewling sounds as though she couldn't even form words to ask me for what she wanted.

"You want me to fuck you?" I asked, and she nodded, her eyes glazed and her mouth opened as I unzipped my pants and took my cock into my hand. I knew there was something I was forgetting, but I didn't care. I just pushed inside of her at once, unable to stop myself as I thrust myself up to the hilt and filled her with my full length.

"Yes, fuck, yes," she groaned, tipping her head back against the pillows and grabbing hold of my shoulders for the leverage to arch her back towards me.

"Good?" I asked, and she nodded again, the ability to talk seeming to have escaped her once more. I liked her like this, unable to hold back, unable to do anything but feel the pleasure that I poured into her. I grabbed her chin and tilted her face up towards me, so I could look into her eyes, and she kissed me once more, reaching down to grab my ass and push me down into her even harder.

I fucked her hard and I fucked her fast, not bothering to hold back; I could feel her warm, slick pussy around me, the way it stretched to make room for me, her tongue in my mouth. I pushed myself up from her again, balancing on my arms so I could drive myself as deep as I could inside of her. Her mouth was slack, her jaw hanging open as though closing it was more muscle control than she had right now. I wanted to commit the sight of her like this to memory. Seeing this woman utterly lost to the pleasure I was giving her was the hottest thing I had ever seen in my life.

"Fuck," she groaned, and she pressed her head into my shoulder, wrapping her arms tight around me and hooking her legs behind my back. It was like she couldn't get enough, like she couldn't even think about getting enough. I knew how she felt. I could have fucked her for the rest of the day if she had let me, not broken for food or water or anything, just feasting myself on her until both of us were totally spent and beyond the point of no return.

I could already feel a tingling in my balls though, a telltale sign that I was getting close – her pussy was perfect, tight around my cock, and I could tell I wouldn't last much longer before I tipped over the edge. She kissed the corner of my mouth, ran her hand through my hair, and groaned – and the sight of her like that in front of me was enough to push me to where I needed to be.

"Mmm," I groaned, as I closed my eyes and felt my cock twitch inside of her, filling her with my sperm. And that seemed to be all she needed to get her there, too – moments later, I felt her tighten around me, and then she let out another groan of pleasure and finished all at once, her body pressed tight to mine, her skin hot and seeming to pass that pleasure from me to her and back again.

Slowly, slowly, after I was sure we were both totally done, I slid out of her, and I slumped on to the couch behind her. She brought her knees to her chest and closed her eyes for a moment, as though not wanting this moment to end so quickly. I knew how she felt. If this could have gone on forever, and if we could have locked ourselves off from the rest of the world for a while, it would have been just perfect.

But, eventually, she pushed herself upright again and reached for her panties, letting out a little sigh of happiness and beaming at me. I reached out to cup her face in my hand for a moment, just glad to be touching her once more.

"That was perfect," she told me, and she kissed my palm and went to grab her clothes. I would have been happy to just have her lounging about naked the rest of the day, but I supposed that we actually had real life to think of, too. I should have headed into the office, just to check on stuff there, and no doubt she had some writing to take care of, as well.

Pulling on her pants, she grabbed her phone out of her pocket it to check it – and as soon as she did, she froze on the spot.

"What's up?" I asked, buckling my pants once more, too satisfied to think that anything might actually be wrong. But then, slowly, she turned to me, her face so white that it looked as though it could have been the paper that they printed her books on.

"I just got an email from my publisher," she told me, voice tiny. I felt my stomach drop. If she was telling me this, then it had to have something to do with us – with what Adrienne had threatened me with earlier in the day.

"What's wrong?" I asked, and she closed her eyes, head dropping to her chest. And, finally, she said out loud the last words on earth that I wanted to hear from her right now.

"They know."

16

ALICIA

"Oh my God, oh my God, oh my God," I muttered as I walked back and forth over the floor of the apartment.

"What's wrong?" he asked me, getting to his feet and reaching for me. I shook my head.

"I need to deal with this," I replied. "I just...I just don't know what I'm meant to do to deal with this, you know?"

"There's so much you can do to deal with this," he promised me, and he wrapped his arms around me and held me close. "You have nothing to worry about. I swear. I'm going to help you out with this. We have this under control."

I leaned into his shoulder and closed my eyes. Fucking *hell*. I couldn't believe this. His ex-girlfriend...of course his ex-girlfriend had been the one to fuck this up. She had reached out to my publisher, and she had told them, without a shadow of a doubt, that there was someone else involved with the writing of those books that had made them so much money.

I was pretty sure that it was only they who knew about it so far. Which was something, at least – I had no idea if there was something that I should do, if I should just email them and tell them that there was nothing to what they had been told. That

Adrienne was a vindictive ex who was just doing this to get back at the man who had rejected her after she had fucked him over.

But they would already have started looking into this. There was a whole lot of information out there about Cameron, about Matt, about everything that they had done together, and if they put even a couple of those pieces into place, they would know that Adrienne was telling the truth. And that I had been holding out on the truth behind my stories all along.

I couldn't believe that I had pulled him into this right alongside me. Right after he had come back and told me that he wanted to stick with me – that things between us were worth fighting for, at least for now. And I was so sure, so certain that there was something honest blooming between us. It was going to be hard, sure, but as long as we had each other, we could figure this out. Couldn't we?

"How are you so calm about this?" I asked Cameron, squeezing on to him tight, glad that he was here to help me through this mess. He knew more about public relations that I did – shit, I was just a writer who liked to sit around and work wrapped up in a towel fresh out of the shower. He was the one with a real business, the one who knew how to handle this stuff.

The one, I reminded myself, with the most to lose. If this got out, to the business world at large, what would people think of him? I knew that the world had a hard time accepting that romance literature was anything other than cheesy fluff for girls who couldn't find time for boyfriends of their own, and so relied on what they could get from fiction instead. It wasn't the sort of thing, in short, that a man like him would be associated with, not really. And I didn't know what sort of impact it could have on his career. There was no precedent for this; no, I was the only idiot who had been foolish enough to drag the man I was falling for into the middle of a huge mess that I hadn't even begun to wrap my head around yet.

"I don't know," Cameron admitted, with a long sigh. "But maybe we can get ahead of this, right? Now that we know that the publisher knows about it. I doubt that they're going to be in any rush to get it out there..."

"Yeah, but we know that she's willing to put this stuff out there," I pointed out. "Who else do you think she's told? That we just haven't heard from yet?"

"Shit, I didn't even think about that," he confessed, and he leaned his forehead against mine for a moment, closing his eyes and taking a deep breath. "I think I need to get out of here and figure out what we're going to do next, okay? I have no idea who she might have told. And who they might have told. And if anyone actually believes her yet..."

"Let's hope that she's as untrustworthy to everyone else as she is to you, right?" I replied, and he let out a little chuckle – even though I knew that he had to be hurting right now, it meant so much to me to hear that laugh come out of his mouth. It felt as though my entire heart swelled when I heard him happy, no matter how brief it might have been, no matter how much of a mess we found ourselves in right now. I was clinging to him for support, floating there in the middle of the ocean. I had no idea how we were going to weather this storm, but maybe that was just what I needed right now. Him. In the middle of this whole mess.

"Okay," he murmured, and he pulled back and planted a kiss on my lips. "We can figure this out, alright? We need to do some damage control. Trust me, I've done stuff like this before."

"Oh, yeah?" I replied, feeling a little more hopeful.

"Yeah, you should have seen the mess that Matt made of the product launch we did last spring," he replied. "I had to work my ass off just to make sure that we didn't get stuck with losing all our clients. Trust me, I can handle this."

"Thank you," I murmured. "If there's anything I can do..."

"Actually, there is," he replied. "Email your publishers, tell them that you want to talk about this in person as soon as you can. That means that they're going to hold off on sharing anything, because they think you have part of the story that they're going to need if they're going to tell it properly."

"Please tell me that I don't have to actually see anyone in person," I protested, with a smile. "You know that I spend all my time in this apartment – there's a reason I avoid speaking to actual real-life people, you know?"

"You think you can manage it for me?" he replied, and I felt my heart soften at once. Because he could have said anything to me in that moment, and I would have nodded along with it and told him that anything he wanted from me, I would at least try. I could handle a meeting with the people who had made my books a success, right?

"I think I can," I promised him. "What are you going to do now?"

"I'm going to get to the office, and make sure that Adrienne hasn't decided to share it with anyone else there," he replied. "I know that Matt might have figured it out, but he knows that it's going to hurt him as much as it will me. Anyone else gets hold of it, and they'll be a ticking time bomb."

"You're right," I agreed. But I didn't want to let go of him. He was like a buffer between this and the real world, between this and actually having to handle the mess that I had made.

"Okay, you can deal with this, okay?" he promised me. "I know you can. If you can write those books, then you can handle everything that comes with it."

"And if not, then I can just write the two of us a new identity," I suggested. He laughed again.

"I always liked the idea of being a fishing captain," he remarked. "You think you could make that happen for me?"

"I'm sure I could write you into another one of my books, but it would be quite a pivot from where you were before," I giggled. Even the thought of him standing on the edge of a fishing boat and gazing out across the ocean, chewing on a pipe and wrapped up in some wet-weather gear, turned me on.

"Yeah, and I think that this is what got us in this mess in the first place," he replied. "So maybe hold off on putting me in another book just yet, okay?"

"I'll see what I can do," I promised him. "I'll get in touch with the publisher, okay, you go and handle what you have to do. Anything that I can do to help out, just let me know, I'll be there in a minute, alright?"

"Alright," he replied, and he kissed me on the forehead again. "I'm going to get out of here. I'll see you soon, okay?"

"I'll see you soon," I replied, and with that, I watched as he walked to the door and waved him off. I managed to keep the smile on my face until it shut behind him, and, as soon as he was gone, I slumped down against the couch and put my head into my hands.

I was shaking slightly. I couldn't believe I had dragged him into this. It just wasn't fair. Not just on him, but on me, too – it felt like I had finally found the guy I actually wanted to be with, and the universe was just tossing a bunch of bullshit in my direction to make it as hard as possible for me to follow through on it. I had heard of exes stirring up shit before, but this was way beyond anything I could have even invented. Especially since she had cheated on him, and should have been slinking away from this with her tail between her legs...

But maybe that was the way it had to be. I thought back to all the romance books I had written, all the ones I had read, and they all had one thing in common – that it wasn't easy. If it were easy, it wouldn't be a story worth telling, would it? Sometimes, you had to put up a fight to be with the person that you loved, even if it was – Love.

It was the first time that I had thought of him in those terms. My entire body seized for a moment, as though the sheer power of that word was more than I could handle all by myself. Did I love him? We had hardly been together for a month, and yet, the depth of my feeling made me sure. I had known him for so long, I had cared for him for so long, I had even lived with him, too – all that had been missing was the physical side of the relationship, and now that it was in place, I had everything I needed to know I was in love with him.

I went to my computer and pulled up a new email to send to my publisher. I had to make this sound as solid and certain as I could. To give us time to work out what we were going to do next. I had to make sure they weren't going to go anywhere else with this information – not that I thought they would, but still.

Anything I could do to rescue us from this mess, I could do it. *I could do it.* He seemed confident we could get through this, and maybe I just needed to take on some of that attitude. At the other side of this, there was a life with a man that I knew I wanted to be with. A man that I had written into fiction, he was so perfect. And a man that I wasn't going to let go of, not for anything.

17

CAMERON

"Cameron!"

A voice called my name as soon as I stepped through the door into the enormous building that housed my office – and as soon as I heard it, my heart sank. Because I knew that this was going to be anything but good news.

Slowly, and with a pit of dread in my stomach, I turned around and saw Matt marching towards me. He had a face like thunder and seemed as though he was ready to toss aside anyway who dared to get in his way at that moment.

"What is it?" I asked, crossing my arms over my chest, trying not to allow my anger at him to show through. We were out here around other people, after all, and the last thing we needed right now was for someone else to catch onto the mess that was going down between the two people who were meant to be keeping this place together.

"You didn't hear already?" he shot back angrily. "Seems like everyone knows your little secret. Now, the only question is, did you put it out there, or did Adrienne break the news?"

"I don't know what you're talking about," I snapped back, and I turned to look over my shoulder to make sure that nobody was listening in to us. Okay, so somebody knew what was going down – but that didn't mean the whole office had to get a front-row seat.

"Okay, let me fill you in," he replied, and he pulled his phone from his pocket and thrust it out in my direction. I took it from him and looked down at the article that he had pulled up on the screen. And as soon as I saw it, my heart sank.

It was about me – just in some stupid gossip magazine, but one that was well-read enough that I could be sure that it wouldn't fly under the radar. There was a picture of me at the top, from some fancy event I had been forced to show my face at for the benefit of the company recently. Shit, shit, shit. And the story? Well, the story was all about the scandalous nature of the books that had been based right on me.

"Adrienne," I growled. And I swear, if she had been in front of me right then and there, I would have dragged her out of the place by her collar myself. She had promised me, at least, that she was going to give me some time before she broke this story. But that had been a bluff. She had put it all out there, and now I had to deal with what was left.

"She told everyone, huh?" Matt demanded, as he took his phone back from me and steered me towards the nearest office room where we could get some privacy.

"Yeah, it looks like it," I admitted. "Alicia got an email from her publisher about it, but I thought that Adrienne might have told just them."

"Seems like we didn't get so lucky," Matt replied, shaking his head. As soon as he had the door shut behind him, he turned his attention to me, and locked his eyes to mine.

"You need to be honest with me, Cam," he told me. It was the first time I'd heard him use that nickname for me in a while, and it surprised me a little, even though I knew that it shouldn't.

"Were you cheating on Adrienne with that chick?" he asked. I shook my head.

"You know I would never have done anything like that," I replied, and I looked him dead in the eye to make sure that he believed what was coming out of my mouth. He knew me. He might have fucked me over. But he still *knew* me. And there was no way he was going to believe that I could lie to him when there was so much on the line.

"You know Adrienne," I reminded him. "You know what she's like. She's vindictive. Don't make me go over everything that she did to fuck me over. This is just another step in all of that, you must see that by now."

He sighed. And I knew that I was finally getting through to him. There was still anger between us, the lingering remainder of the betrayal of what had happened between us, but at least we were on the same side here. Working for the same thing.

"I don't think I have any choice but to believe you now," he confessed, shaking his head. The wall that had been up between us seemed to have softened a little. I didn't know how long it would last, but shit, I needed someone on my side who could make all this shit go away.

"Yeah, I don't think so," I agreed grimly. "What are we going to do about this? What are the articles saying? How many people know by now?"

"I don't know, but I saw at least a half-dozen articles about it," he replied with a sigh. "Mostly just light entertainment pieces and a couple of pieces on literary gossip blogs, but…"

"Literary gossip blogs?" I repeated after him. "I didn't even know that was a thing."

"Yeah, tell me about it," he chuckled. For a moment, it was like things had always been this way between us – that nothing had happened to drive that wedge in between Matt and me.

"But they exist, and they're one of the places covering this," he replied. "People are matching up timelines, the whole thing. I've been thinking about how we can spin it, but I've got a few ideas."

"Hit me with them," I replied. "I'll do anything I can to make this go away."

"You're actually dating this girl now, right?" he asked me. I hesitated for a moment before I replied. I didn't even know if we were officially dating or not yet, but after I had gone down there to tell her that I wanted to be with her, I supposed it was as close to official as to make no odds. Being caught up in a public scandal together was the same thing as actually dating, wasn't it?

"Yeah, I think so," I replied. He nodded.

"Okay, so I think that's our best course of action to spin this thing," he explained. "Lean into it, yeah? It might not look great for us, but if we can sell this idea that she's just so in love with you that she couldn't help but write all these stories about you, we can work a more wholesome angle into it. And we'll just have to hope that nobody we work with in the future actually thinks to read any of those books."

"Oh, come on, you know that nobody in this industry reads anything more than what they think will sound good when they bring it up at dinner parties," I pointed out, and he snorted with amusement.

"Yeah, I know," he conceded. "Still, we just make sure that we try to keep the actual name of the books as vague as possible. As far out of these stories as possible. You get it?"

"I get it."

"Good, because you're going to need to get her on board with this," he replied. "Do you know who publishes her books? Because if you can find out, I can get in touch with them, offer to get the article placed in some big magazines – I'm sure they'd be happy with the promo, especially if it's for free…"

He was off now, talking almost to himself, bouncing ideas off the walls. All of them sounded good to me. Honestly, anything that would get the spotlight off me as soon as possible was everything I needed right now. I knew that I would have to lean into it for a little while, just to make sure that we had control of the narrative, but after that, if everything went according to plan, then we could leave all this behind us and forget that it had ever happened.

"Matt," I cut him off, and he blinked and looked down at me, as though he had half-forgotten that I was there.

"Yeah?"

"I just wanted to say," I replied, and I took a deep breath, not quite sure that I was actually going to come out with what I wanted to say next. "Thank you. For all of this. I know this is a huge mess, and I couldn't get through it without you. I'm sorry I dumped the company in the middle of this, and I promise that I'll try to keep you in the loop with anything like this in the future, so it doesn't come as a surprise."

"Shit, man, you have other romance franchises that you're the secret leading man of?" he remarked, with a grin. "Because I had hoped that I would only have to deal with this one time."

I smiled back at him – I couldn't help but remember Alicia's little comment when we had been back at her apartment, about writing us whole new identities so we could start over again. But I shook my head.

"No, as far as I know, it's just this one," I replied. "Once this is done with, you'll never have to deal with it again."

"Deal?" he replied, sticking his hand out to mine.

"Deal," I replied, and I took it. And, for a moment, it was like everything that had happened between us had just blinked out of existence. Yes, this asshole had still been the one who had been hooking up with my fiancée behind my back – but he was also the one who would cover me when I needed help, who would spin the story when I had no idea how to save face in light of something I could never have planned for. Sure, the two of us were interlocked, so anything that happened to me would affect him, too, but he could have tried to play this to get rid of me once and for all. Instead, he was making sure I was going to get out of this, with as little skid left on my backtrack as possible.

"Okay, I'm going to go and get out of here, see how many places I can get to take down their stories," he replied. "You get in touch with her, alright? Ask her to help us out on this. She got you into this mess, she can sure as hell get you out of it."

"I will," I replied, and with that, he turned on his heel and walked out of there. As soon as the door was shut behind him, I rubbed my hands over my face and wondered how all of this could have happened in just one day. I couldn't believe that Adrienne had managed to turn a nuclear bomb against my life, detonate it, and then run off to leave me to deal with the fallout. Thank God I had people on my side who could help me. I hadn't even spoken to Alicia about it yet, but I knew that she would be glad to help me out with this any way she could – she had been beating herself up about it enough that I knew she would jump at the chance to fix it.

I almost felt a little sorry for Adrienne, really. Because she had come out here to try to ruin my life, because she had nothing she wanted left in hers. Well, little did she know that I had people who cared about me. People who would work with me. People who were here to make sure she couldn't take anything else from me. She had already made a mess of my life, but she wasn't going to get a chance to do it again.

I was going to take this on. And I was going to win.

18

ALICIA

"You look beautiful," Cameron assured me, as he slipped an arm around my shoulders, pulling me close to him, and I looked at myself in the mirror again and winced.

"I don't know," I replied, as I touched the scarlet-red lip that they had given me and tried not to fiddle with the ridiculously overblown curls that were piled on top of my head. "You don't think it's a bit...much?"

I felt as though that was a bit of an understatement, really. But there wasn't much I could do about it, given that the shoot was starting any moment now and I couldn't ask them to redo my makeup this late in the game.

I still couldn't believe I was actually going to be a cover model. Well, okay, not the cover, but there would at least be a full-page spread of me with my man on my arm to accompany the giant story they were writing about us. The interviewer had paced back and forth between us in Cameron's gorgeous penthouse apartment, hitting us with apparently every question that passed through her head, about the background to our relationship, when I had started writing the books, when I had figured out the two of us were *meant* to be together. That's how she kept putting it, no matter how much I protested her use of that language – that we were *meant* to be, and the fact that we were finally official was just a universal inevitability that had finally come to pass.

I had agreed to this because it seemed like the only way I could make sure to fix the mess I had made with my stories and of our lives. It had been Cameron's business partner's idea, and it had sounded like the best thing I could think of to put an end to this. When I had reached out to my publisher, they had been on board with it, glad for the chance to get their books in front of a whole new audience, and I just hoped this would be enough to paper over the cracks of what I had done in the first place.

But actually going through with it? That was something else altogether. I wasn't used to this much scrutiny; sure, I had done a couple of meet-ups here and there, and I had managed to keep my shit together and not look like too much of an idiot for a couple of hours at a time. But I had no idea if I could manage to pull off something that would come under the scrutiny of however-the-fuck-many people were going to see me in this magazine.

"You're going to be fine," Cameron soothed me. "You look beautiful, really. I love this look on you."

"Well, don't get used to it," I warned him. "I don't think I can ever pull this off again. Not sure that I want to, either…"

And I wasn't lying. They had me in this amazing body-con red dress, with my hair teased up to at least four inches around my whole head; my makeup was dark and way over-the-top, with dark red lips and a smoky eye that would have taken me at least a half-dozen attempts to get right. They told me they were going for the look of a romance novel heroine, and I guessed I sort of fit that archetype, but it just didn't feel like me.

"It's going to be over soon," Cameron promised me. "Not long now."

"And we can go out and get fries after, right?" I asked. "Because I don't know how much longer I can keep holding my stomach in under this shapewear."

"More fries than you can eat," he replied, and he kissed me on the forehead.

"Oh, you two are so cute together!" One of the set assistants sighed as she walked past us, and I pulled back from him a little nervously. There was something strange about the two of us being so public with one another; things between us were so new, and I was still trying to work out just how I felt about him, and coming under public scrutiny in the midst of all that just made my head feel like a mush.

"Not long till this is over," I repeated, mostly to myself. I looked over at Cameron in the mirror; he had gotten to wear this gorgeous suit, and he looked so handsome that I could have swooned just glancing in his direction. He was totally rocking this cool billionaire bad-boy thing – maybe because I just so happened to have based the very character who fit that mold upon him.

"Are you guys ready to start the shoot?" the photographer, a guy in his thirties who looked as though he wanted to be anywhere but here right now, asked us as he looked down at the little viewfinder on his camera.

"Yeah, I think so," I replied nervously, and Cameron squeezed me tight.

"Yeah, we're ready," Cameron replied with more confidence.

"Alright, come over to the set, and just...I don't know, do what feels right," the photographer replied, and he guided us over to the fancy office setup that had been put together specifically for this shoot. I couldn't help but smirk when I saw the desk sitting there in front of us. It looked more than a little like the one I had blown him beside in his own office. Did they know about that here? I had no idea. Probably not. And if they did, they were really pushing it with a reference as cheeky as this one.

"Okay, what if I start here..." Cameron asked, and he shifted me to the front of the desk so that my whole body was on display. The dress was so short, I could practically feel the bite of air on my bare butt. I hoped that I wasn't showing off anything too scandalous. I hadn't told anyone about this shoot, but it was going out in a pretty popular magazine, so there was a chance that someone I knew could see it, and I would have preferred to be looking at least decent if nothing else.

The photographer and the set designer maneuvered the two of us around the set, this way and that, getting us to pose close to each other like we were the cover models for some romance novel. And honestly, at a certain point, I found myself loosening up and having a little fun; I wouldn't have been able to do it if I had been with anyone other than him, but with Cameron there to help me through it, it was actually kind of a good time.

"You okay in those heels?" he asked, as I wobbled and leaned on his shoulder between shots. I shook my head.

"Not at all," I replied. "But I'm going to be out of them soon enough, so don't worry about it."

"You need me to put you on my shoulders?" he joked. "Make sure you don't fall over?"

"Hey, I'm not sure that's really the vibe they're going for here," I replied. "That's more scout camp than sexy romance stuff..."

"Maybe you could write that into your new book, so we had a reason to pose for it now," he pointed out, and I giggled.

"Right alongside those stories where you're a fisherman and I'm a fish?" I replied, and he shook his head at me fondly.

"I never said that you were a fish," he replied. "You'd be...I don't know. The boat?"

"I'm pretty sure you just insulted me," I warned him. "But I'm willing to let it go for now, if you keep reminding me about the fries we're going to get after this."

"Sorry to interrupt," the photographer commented sarcastically, clearly not giving one little damn about the fact he was sticking his nose in between us.

"You ready to get back to shooting?" he asked, and I nodded, feeling a little flush to my cheeks, as though I had been caught out in the act.

It didn't take long before the shoot was finally over and done with, and I headed straight back to the wardrobe department so I could get changed into the jeans and sweater I had come here in. I scrubbed the layers of makeup off my face and went out to meet Cameron, who was talking with the interviewer again. But when he saw me, he stopped at once, and grinned widely in my direction.

"Well, hello," he replied.

"Bet you didn't recognize me without all that shit on my face," I joked, but I was suddenly feeling a little insecure. I knew it was ridiculous, but what if he liked me better that way? I didn't know if I could just come out and ask him, but the question thrummed at the back of my mind. He was used to glamour, to the expensive things in life. Should I have made more of an effort to fit in to that myself?

"You look perfect," he replied, and he dropped a kiss on my forehead and put his arms around my waist, pulling me in close to him and smiling down at me happily.

"Thank you," I replied, and I felt like I had been gifted something so special and so precious I could hardly wrap my head around it. Maybe we had been meant for this, after all. Maybe there was something to that, no matter how much I wanted to be a cynic about it.

There was this place not far from where we had been shooting, a little diner that served mountains of fries with amazing sauces and dips, and that was all I was craving as soon as we were done. We walked down there together, hand in hand, and he seemed like he was unwilling to let go of me for even a second. I knew how he felt. There was a comfort to having him beside me, even though I knew all of this was still a mess, a work-in-progress. I would figure out a way to get through it with him there, and I knew that. Or at least, I could believe it when he was standing beside me.

"Oh my God, I've been looking forward to this all day," I groaned, as soon as the food arrived in front of us and I started to tuck in. I was so hungry and so antsy from having to keep my stomach sucked in all day that I was pretty sure I could have inhaled ten platefuls of the food in an instant. I sipped on the milkshake that I had gotten to go with it, and then ducked one of my fries into the frothy, tasty chocolate sludge.

"I'm glad it's over with," Cameron agreed, as he bit into his burger and sipped on the coffee he had ordered to go with it. I didn't know how he could just drink coffee like that at any time of the day – I would have been up all night if I had allowed myself to send that much caffeine pulsing around my system, but that was just how he seemed to function. It was something that I hadn't noticed when the two of us had been friends, but now that we were something more than that, I felt as though I could see him in a whole new light.

"Now we just have to wait and find out if it worked, huh?" I remarked, and he nodded. Reaching over the table, he squeezed my hand tight, and looked intently into my eyes.

"I know that it will," he told me firmly. "And then all of this is over with, okay? And we can go back to reality."

"And what does reality look like after all of this?" I wondered aloud. He shrugged and shook his head.

"I have to admit, I don't know yet," he conceded. "But it's going to be good. I promise you that."

And, as I sat there opposite him at that table, tucked into the corner booth of a tiny diner in the middle of the city, I couldn't help but smile. Because if he thought it was going to be good – then I knew it was going to be great.

19

CAMERON

I flicked through the pages of the magazine, the one that contained the story about Alicia and me, and I couldn't keep the smile off my face.

It had just arrived this morning, and I had rushed to check it out as soon as I'd gotten the chance. I knew that everything hinged on this – that if we were going to sell all the stuff that we wanted to sell, we needed to know that this story had come out well. The interviewer had seemed pretty taken with us, but that didn't mean anything, not really. She could have written anything about us, if we weren't careful, and I refused to spend any more of my time worrying about it now the story was out at last.

And, much to my relief – there it was. Printed in black and white. This incredibly positive, actually kind of sweet retelling of our relationship, a little human-interest story with a flair for the dramatic, just like we had been promised. The pictures of us hanging off one another on that set they had put together for us were a little silly, but that had been the point. They were never the ones I would have chosen to represent us, but they were going for something that was a little closer to the fantasy of our relationship they had been trying to sell in this story. It was perfect. Exactly what I had been hoping for. I knew I would still have to wait to make sure that everyone felt the same way about it that I did, but for now, I was pretty sure that everything had gone just the way I wanted it to.

Jesus Christ, it was a relief to know that the worst of it was over. Okay, I knew there would still be a few details to figure out here and there, still a few corners to fold down and edges to smooth out to make sure that nobody got the wrong idea about what this meant for the business – like Matt had said, it seemed unlikely that anyone we would work with would give much of a damn about this, because most of them never picked up a book unless it promised to make them richer, but still. At least this was finally under our control again. At least the narrative was where we wanted it to be.

There was a knock on the door, and a moment later, before I'd had a chance to respond, Matt entered the room, holding the same magazine that I had been flicking through. He waved it in the air happily, as though it was a victory banner.

"Looks like we pulled it off, huh?" he remarked, and I nodded.

"Looks like we did," I agreed. "You did a good job, Matt. I don't think I'd ever have been able to pull off something like this."

"Yeah, well, that's what I'm here for," he pointed out. "To clean up any messes that spring up around these parts, right?"

"Something like that," I agreed, and he grinned at me.

"You know, you really sold it in these pictures," he remarked. "The two of you look like you're totally in love."

I chuckled, but the word made something ping at the back of my mind.

"Yeah, well, we had a good photographer," I replied. "He knew how to get what he wanted out of us."

"I guess I just had no idea that Alicia could look like that," he remarked, and his eyes were pinned to the page once more – I felt a stir of irritation at him, a reminder that whatever had happened between us, I sure as hell wasn't going to be forgetting what he had done to me just a few weeks before.

"Yeah, I think you should stop looking at her like that," I told him bluntly. "I know what you're like with the women I'm dating now – I'm not letting you anywhere near her."

Matt sighed, and for a moment, it looked as though he was going to protest. But then, instead, he held his hands up, and closed the magazine once more.

"Fair enough," he conceded, and he looked to his watch. "Will you be at the meeting at twelve? I want to check in with a few of the international clients, find out how far this news has gotten."

"Yeah, of course I will," I assured him, and he nodded.

"Alright, see you then."

And with that, he backed out of the room and left me to it once more. Though exactly what *it* was, I wasn't quite certain about one way or another. I looked down at the magazine once more, at the pictures of the two of us that were in front of me, and I wondered if what Matt had said to me was true. If we really did look as though we were in love.

Not that I had any great problem with looking like it, of course. Because at least that meant people would believe there was less of the sordid about it and more of the romantic. But because...well, because I didn't know if that was actually how she felt about me or not. Or if that was how I'd felt about her. When this had started, it had just been fun, something for us to enjoy after I had been through a rough breakup and so I didn't have to bother going back out on the dating scene to get back in the game again, and because she was newly single, too. Not something that led to anything like love. Not as far as I was concerned.

But the lines had blurred more quickly than I had been able to take control of, and now I knew I wanted to be around her more than anything else in the world right now. When you already had that groundwork of the friendship in place, it felt like the warmth of what we had spread a little faster and grew a little easier than it might have done if we were just starting out from zero. We already had that easy banter, that chemistry outside of the bedroom. When I went out for dinner with her, like we did at the diner after the shoot, it was just like hanging out with my best friend. But then, we got to go home afterwards, and when we were in bed together, it was like exploring someone brand new for the very first time.

That was a dangerous mix, I was coming to realize. One that was more potent than I had given it credit for. Because when I looked at her, not just at the shoot but in the real world, too, I supposed that I did it with love. It might not have been the full-blown romantic love I was ready to shout from the rooftops, but it was there, no doubt in my mind. I wanted to be with her, that was for sure, but maybe I was moving too fast, even inside my own head? Maybe I should have pulled back a little, remembered that I had just gotten out of a messy engagement and I didn't want to dive head-first into something so serious.

But when I thought about her, I knew that there would be no denying the reality of the way I felt. I wanted her. Even through all the mess that had been caused by the two of us getting together, I wanted her. Nothing could stop that, nothing could change that, nothing could convince me that it was anything other than the right choice for the both of us. It might have been more than we had been prepared for, but it didn't mean it was wrong. It just meant that I had to find some way to adapt to this new state of being, so I could be the best partner to her I possibly could be.

I stared down at the pictures for another moment, and suddenly felt the deep craving for the sound of her voice once more. I picked up the phone and dialed her number, drumming my fingers on the desk as I waited for her to pick up.

"Hello?" she greeted me, after a few rings, sounding sleepy as she answered the call.

"Sorry, did I wake you up?" I asked.

"Yeah, but you shouldn't be sorry about it," she replied, blearily, letting out a big yawn. "I needed to get up anyway. And you're a nicer alarm call than my usual one."

"Good," I replied, with a chuckle. "Hey, did you see the magazine's come out today? The one with our story in it?"

"Oh, shit, really, was that today?" she exclaimed. "I didn't know it was going to be so soon, I thought we had a while to wait yet..."

"No, I'm holding a copy of it right now," I replied. "And the story's great. You should get a copy of it to take a look at when you have a chance, I think you'll be really happy with what they put out there."

"I sure hope so," she agreed, letting out another yawn. "You think it's going to be enough to make sure none of this goes any further?"

"I'd be surprised if it wasn't," I replied, with a nod, even though she couldn't see me. "I don't see what anyone else could want from this story that wasn't already covered here, and I think that's the most important thing."

"Jesus, you have no idea how much of a relief it is to hear you say that," she remarked. "This is all over now, right? We don't have to worry about Adrienne trying to pull anything else out of the back of the closet to make us look like idiots?"

"No, it's all over," I promised her. "I think this calls for a celebration. You want to go out to dinner tonight? I know a place not far from your apartment, it's small, but they have great food, and the wine's cheap, too."

"God, you really know how to romance a girl." She laughed. "That sounds perfect. What time do you want to meet there?"

"Shall we say seven?" I replied. "I have some stuff to take care of here before I can head out for the day, but if that works for you...?"

"Yeah, seven works for me," she agreed at once. "Thanks for the alarm call again, by the way. I should hire you full-time to wake me up in the mornings."

"Anytime," I replied, and I found myself lingering at the other end of the line, thinking of all the stuff I wanted to say to her, everything that just felt as though it was on the tip of my tongue and begging to come out.

But that could wait, at least for now. I had other stuff to take care of, and I wasn't going to let myself get caught up in everything I planned to share with her. I would see her soon, and I could tell her everything that was running through my head when it came around.

"I'll see you soon," I promised her, and with that, I hung up the phone...before I wasted the rest of the day on the phone with the woman who just so happened to be my best friend, my lover, all wrapped up in one. And I started counting down the seconds until I would get a chance to see her again. Because it was never soon enough for my liking.

20

ALICIA

"Shh," I tried to shush Cameron, but I was giggling so hard it was difficult to keep my voice down. The two of us tumbled over the threshold to my apartment, and I hung on to him for dear life, a little too tipsy on the wine I had put away at dinner to think about anything other than how badly I wanted him.

The magazine had come out earlier that day, with the story about us, and it had been perfect – I'd read it twice all the way through and stared at the photos of the two of us together, wondering who in the hell the glamorous woman was and if she had actually been inside me all the time. I decided, in honor of the release, I should at least make some kind of effort for the date we were heading out on, and I spent an hour teasing my hair and applying makeup to try to recreate the look I had been given in that shoot. Okay, so it could probably still use a little work, but when I saw the look on Cameron's face as I swanned through the door to join him, I knew it had done the job.

"You look incredible," he murmured, as he got to his feet to greet me, planting a kiss on my cheek and making my heart feel like it was going to come busting right out of my chest. How was it that being with him actually felt like romance? I had dated so many guys before him, but none of them had ever made me feel the things that I had written about this whole time. But when I was with Cameron...all of that just seemed to fall away. As though it had always just been us. As though there had never been anyone else.

Dinner was perfect; just the two of us, chatting about the article, toasting to our relief it was finally all over with and that we could go back to reality. The waiter came over and lit a candle between us, the sort of thing I might have rolled my eyes at if I had been with anyone else, but when it came to Cameron, it only felt fair that we indulged ourselves in the most intense romance we could manage.

By the time dinner was over, he had his hand on my leg beneath the table, and I couldn't think about anything other than getting him back to my place so I could get my hands on him once and for all. He held my hand all the way home, as though he wanted to make sure that anyone we passed on the street would know that the two of us were together, and I sure as hell wasn't going to complain. By the time we got to the door, I could feel the needy heat rising up inside of me, and when he planted his lips to the back of my neck as I fumbled with the key, I practically melted on the spot.

We tumbled over the threshold together, and he pulled me against his body and kissed me hard, as though this was what he had been waiting for all day long. I was surprised we had actually managed to make it back to my place; sometimes, it felt like the chemistry between us was just too intense to deny, that I couldn't hold back when I was around him and I just had to have him right there and then.

"God, you look so fucking hot in that dress," he murmured to me, pushing me back against the door and pushing his hands beneath the short hem of the dress that I had slipped into for the evening. His hands gripped tight to my thighs, and he kissed me, his tongue in my mouth as he pushed my legs apart roughly on the spot. Sometimes, I was pretty sure he had been taking notes from my wildest fantasies – and then I remembered he might well have been doing just that. I had written them all into those books, after all, and I knew that he had indulged himself with a few read-throughs here and there...

But soon enough, those thoughts had vanished from my head, as his hand cupped around my panties and traced against my pussy. I was aching for him – there was something about getting all dressed up for him like this that made it hard to control myself, knowing I had put together this look just to be observed and appreciated by him. The whole night through, every time I had seen his gaze dart down to the cleavage that peeped over the top of the dress, whenever I had felt his fingers brush against my leg beneath the table, it had been more than I could take. The foreplay starting before I had so much as gotten him back to my place. It would have been outright indecent, if it weren't so damn hot.

His mouth traced down, over my chin, to my throat, his lips grazing over my pulse so he could feel the intensity of my heart-beat beneath his lips. He knew that it beat for him – only him now – that there was nobody else who came close to doing what he did to me. His touch, the way he held me, the way he kissed me, it was like everything else just seemed to slip-slide out of existence to leave only the two of us in their place.

"Turn around," he breathed into my ear, his voice leaving no room for argument, and I did as I was told at once. He pushed up my dress and yanked down my panties, sinking his fingers into my bare ass for a moment and making me groan. My whole body felt like it was on fire for him, my pussy aching to feel him fill me, and I arched my back and pushed myself back towards him, trying to tell him any way I could that I wanted to feel him inside of me.

I heard the zip of his pants, and then felt the pressure of his cock as he nudged up against my entrance. God, that feeling – I wasn't sure I was ever going to be able to get over how good it felt when he did that to me, how good it felt when I could sense he was as ready for this as I was. One hand was planted on my hip, and my heels had arched me up high enough that he could slide down and into me at any moment he wanted. But he seemed in no rush to push towards that edge – instead, he leaned forward, his mouth right next to my ear, and spoke.

"You want me to fuck you?"

I nodded. Moaned. I didn't know how much more obvious I could have made it.

"Tell me," he ordered me.

"I want you to fuck me," I breathed, at last, and then, finally, I felt him push all the way inside of me. The sound I made as he filled me up sounded something other than human, but I didn't much care. All that mattered to me was this guy wanted me. That this man, this man who meant so much to me, cared for me the same way I cared for him. There was something so dangerous about throwing yourself into something in this way, about plunging over the edge and into real feeling, but I knew that as long as he returned everything I felt for him, I would find a way to make it through. I could do this. I could do this, as long as I had him here to catch me as I was falling.

I pressed my hands to the door in front of me and used the leverage to grind back against his cock. He felt so fucking good inside of me, it almost made me feel like I was drunk on him, every nerve ending in my body shooting off in a hundred different directions as I tried to wrap my head around how he could feel this good right now. He growled with pleasure, a low, hungry noise that told me I was doing something right, and I flicked my gaze over my shoulder to look at him and grinned when I saw the sheer, blatant lust he had aimed in my direction.

But then, he grabbed my hips and started fucking me harder, harder than he had before, harder than anyone ever had, slamming into me so that our hips were clashing together over and over again and all I could hear was the sound of our skin meeting, my labored breath tearing out of my throat.

"You feel so good," he moaned, and he slipped his hand between my legs so he could play with my clit as he fucked me – as soon as I felt his fingers there, my whole body seemed to give in, and I knew I wouldn't be able to last much longer. It was as though every muscle in my body was tensed, tensing, needing that release more than it needed anything else in the world. I wanted this. I needed this. I couldn't handle not having this. I didn't care what it took – I knew I would always come back to him for this kind of pleasure, that nothing would be able to draw me away, to someone else to look for what I knew I could get from him and him alone.

"Fuck, yes," I gasped, and soon enough, I felt that orgasm rising up and through me, threatening to take control of me once more. The edges of my vision were blurred and my heart was pounding so fast it seemed to threaten to come right out of the front of my chest. My body trembled as I arched on the very edge of the release I knew I needed, and then, at last, I felt myself go – tipping towards the edge, helpless, hopeless, crying out so loudly that everyone in my building would have been able to hear me. I didn't care. Let them. Let them know how much I wanted this man. I wanted everyone in the world to hear me right now.

Moments later, I felt him reach his own release inside of me, his cock twitching as he drilled deep into my pussy and filled me up with his seed. He let out a low, throaty groan, and held himself right there for a long instant, freezing the moment in time like there was nothing else he wanted to do, nowhere else in the world he wanted to be.

He pulled out of me and turned me around, kissed me hard – I knew we had just finished, but we were far from done for the night. He pulled back to gaze into my eyes for a moment, and, in that second, I felt such a swell of affection for him. Such a swell it made me forget I had never said the words out loud to him before, and that I didn't know if he was ready to hear them. Such a swell, that they just fell out of me, as though they should have been obvious to anyone who was paying attention.

"I love you," I told him, before I could stop myself. And, as I watched his face crease with surprise, I realized that I had just pushed a button I could never un-push.

21

CAMERON

"I'll see you tomorrow, okay?" I told Alicia, and I leaned down to drop a kiss on her head before I opened the door and slipped out of her apartment. She smiled at me as I went, but I could tell she was nervous, that there was something she wanted to say to me but had no idea how to say it.

And I knew just what was on her mind, too. Everything that had happened over the last few weeks, well, it had been enough to make me forget that the two of us were really building this relationship into something real. It had been such a rush, with everything that needed to get done, with all the stories that people were spinning around us, that it was hard for me to think about anything but moving past that.

And, in that time, she had fallen in love with me, behind my back.

That's what it felt like, anyway. The two of us had just been lying together, gazing into each other's eyes, when she had said it. For a split second, I had considered saying it back, because it just seemed so obvious and so natural and so clear that this was what had to come next. But I stopped myself before I replied. Because I didn't know what I felt for her, if I felt the same as she did – and I didn't want to come out with anything I couldn't take back if the time came, if it was called for.

The rest of the night, those words had seemed to hang between us, impossible to ignore and yet impossible to acknowledge. I had no idea if I should have sat her down and talked to her about all of this seriously. Maybe it would have been better if we'd cleared the air? If I had told her I liked her so much, but I was going to need more time to get used to this new arrangement before I said something like that back to her?

I supposed, for me, it was the fact I had been with someone else so recently. Okay, so now I knew the version of Adrienne I thought I had been in love with didn't exist, but that didn't mean I didn't remember what it was like to say *I love you* to someone else entirely. It just wouldn't have felt right, really, for me to go and blurt that out to someone else when I knew I should have been more careful with my feelings.

I didn't want to get hurt again. That was what it came down to. I didn't want to get hurt again and, in truth, I had no idea if this woman would hurt me if she got the chance. I wanted to believe she would never have done a thing like that, but how could I tell for sure, really? How could I prove it to myself enough for me to say those words back to her, without fearing they were going to be turned around and used against me when I least expected it? I wanted to trust her, I did, but we had spent so long spinning a story about how the two of us were together, it was hard to tell where the fiction had ended and the reality of what we had with each other began.

Shit. I needed to get myself together. I felt like I was going to lose my mind if I spent much more time running all of this through my head. When we had been caught up in the midst of our drama, at least that had been something for me to focus on for a change – I didn't have to think about anything but how it made me feel, how we were going to get through it. But now we were out the other side, and I had to figure out what a relationship with her really looked like.

I walked the rest of the way home and wondered if I should have said something to her when I got the chance. I wished there was something I could do to go back in time and offer the right words in response to what she had said to me. She had gazed at me for a moment, as though she had been waiting for me to come out and say it back, and in that silence, I was just left with the weight of the shock of what I had just heard as I tried to make sense of how I felt about her – and whether I was ready to say it out loud yet.

When I got back to my place, I pulled out my phone and stared down at it for a moment. I needed someone to talk to about this. Normally, I would have called up Alicia and asked her for advice, but that was one of the pains in the ass of dating your best friend, I supposed – you couldn't talk to them about romantic troubles anymore. If I would even describe this as a trouble...

And then, it hit me – Mom. She had spoken to me about Alicia a long time ago, before all of this had even started, when she had first found out that Adrienne had been cheating on me and that things were over between us. She had always liked Alicia, and I knew she had often wondered why I didn't give things a try with her. Well, now I had – and now I needed someone around to help me figure out what the hell I was going to do about our relationship now that it seemed to have taken such a step forward all of a sudden.

I dialed her number and leaned back on my couch as I waited for her to answer. I knew I was going to have to deal with a little bit of her crowing with triumph that she had been right about Alicia all along, but I could handle it, as long as I got some advice on what I was meant to do next. She answered after a few rings, and, before I could so much as come out with anything, she had started to assault me with questions.

"What's going on with you and that story in the magazine?" she asked. "Are you and Alicia really together? Is it something to do with your work? Why didn't you say anything…"

"Hey, Mom," I greeted her, with a chuckle, and she fell silent for a moment, allowing me to take the lead.

"Yeah, it's real," I admitted. "I'm sorry I didn't tell you about it before. Things have been kind of crazy down here since it all started; I didn't really have a chance to stop and fill anyone else in on what's been going on."

"Why? What's been happening?" she asked worriedly. I sighed. I didn't even know where to start. And I didn't know if I could get through this story without having to tell my own mother about the part where I got a blowjob from my girlfriend at work, though I would do my level best to skip over that part of it for now.

I caught her up on everything that had been happening as best I could – I knew it must have sounded crazy, really, but it wasn't like I was sharing anything with her that wasn't true. I just needed help. I knew she would have something useful to say to me, and I was even more certain that time was ticking out on how long I could wait before I came back to Alicia with an answer to her feelings from me.

"So…the two of you really are together now?" she asked.

"Yeah, we are," I admitted. "I didn't expect it, but it worked out that way. I'm happy about it, too – I think that we're a good match and everything; things are going well."

"But?" she prompted me, too motherly not to notice the fact that I was holding something back from her in that moment. I sighed again.

"But, she just told me that she loved me for the first time," I admitted. "And…well, it feels like things haven't been over that long with Adrienne and me, you know? I'm not sure I'm ready to say it back to her yet. But I don't want her to think that I'm dodging the question, or something."

She fell silent for a moment, as though she was taking in the extent of everything I had just said to her. I knew she would have some hot-off-the-press opinions on it, but I needed someone who could help me understand what I was feeling. Maybe even someone to just give me the permission I needed to work through those feelings, to embrace them in their entirety.

"You really like her, don't you?" she asked.

"I really do," I admitted. "But I'm worried. Is it too fast? I was going to get married to someone else just a couple of months ago; I don't know if I should be letting myself think about getting seriously involved with someone else, not yet. I don't want to jump into something else too quickly and ruin what could be a good thing, you know?"

"Who says that you're going to ruin it?" she remarked, sounding surprised. "I know it's not ideal, but sometimes, love isn't. I know it might not make sense to you – you're all business, I know that – but Alicia is a good fit for you. I've been saying it for years. I'd have said it on the day you were meant to get married to Adrienne, if you'd have let me."

I laughed.

"I don't doubt it for a second," I replied. The thought of her rolling up on my wedding day to matter-of-factly tell me I was marrying the wrong woman was so completely on-brand for her, it was almost funny. I knew she totally would have done it, too, if she thought she could stop me making a mistake I couldn't go back from.

"Yes, exactly," she replied. "And this might not have come around at the perfect time for you, but love doesn't always work like that. Sometimes, you've just got to take what is given to you when it's given to you. That's what the universe wants from you."

I pulled a face.

"And I know that you think all that fate talk is just silliness," she continued, as though she could somehow see through the phone and to my grimace of disbelief. "But maybe you should open yourself up to it a little. You never know where it's going to get you."

"I guess not," I confessed. It was something I had hated the idea of for so long, and I had no intention of just jumping in and forgetting everything I believed in, all the logic I had built my life around. But perhaps, just perhaps, she had a point. Maybe I had to let go of some of the control I had been hanging onto for dear life all this time, and accept that something good had been dropped into my life. And that I was going to have to fight to keep it there, as much as humanly possible.

"Thanks, Mom," I replied, and I meant it. "Thanks a lot. I need…I think I need some time to think."

"Don't take too long," she warned me. "Women like Alicia don't wait around forever."

"I won't," I promised her. And I meant it. Because I knew she was right. Alicia had already waited long enough for me. And, now that we had finally given in and found one another, there was no way in hell I was going to let her slip through my fingers. I just had to find the perfect way to say it back to her. The perfect way to fit the perfect man she had made me into in her stories. And soon, my mind was racing with ideas – of everything I would do to her when I got the chance, and everything I would give her once I had said those three little words back.

22

ALICIA

I PACED THE APARTMENT, FEELING LIKE I WAS GOING TO EXPLODE IF I didn't work off some of the excess energy rushing through my system in that moment.

How was it that just saying those words out loud was enough to flick a switch inside of me? That not hearing them back right away had sent me spinning through a hopeless mess in my head? I needed to get a handle on myself, but I had no idea what that looked like right about now, and I needed someone to come in and tell me everything was going to be just fine.

But the only person who could do that had walked out of this place a few hours before, and I knew that now wasn't the time to go looking for him to get what I knew I needed so badly. He'd clearly been a little shocked when I had said those words to him, and I knew I had overstepped my mark.

It felt like those words had just slipped out of my mouth before I'd had a chance to get hold of them. I knew I should have been more careful, but it was so difficult when I just wanted him to know how I felt about him. I had been waiting long enough for him to come into my life – not as my friend, but as my lover, as everything I had ever wanted in a man. Now that he was here, it only felt right that I tell him everything I had felt for him all this time, everything I had felt before I had even known I felt it for him...

Shit. I needed to distract myself, or else I was just going to spend the rest of the day wandering around this place and trying to work out what I could do to fix the mess I had made. If I had made a mess at all? It was hard to tell, not as if I could just straight up ask him *Hey, so, did my saying I love you scare the shit out of you or were you just doing a really good impression of that?*

I went to my computer, booted it up, and drummed my fingers on my leg as I waited for it to come to life in front of me. Maybe I could do some writing? Sometimes, when I was having a hard time working through the feelings in my head, I found it useful to turn to the page, to just pour all of it out onto there and hope it made me feel better. I checked my emails first – and, to my surprise, there was a message from the publisher sitting there.

I skimmed through it quickly, and, to my surprise, they were already getting back to me about the pages I had submitted a few days before – the ones I had written when Cameron had told me we should slow things down and take a break for the time being, when I had felt like my whole world was falling apart and there was nothing I could do to slow it down or stop it. When I had written my characters with the sadness I had felt, because it seemed unfair for them to get to enjoy themselves when I felt like my own heart had been ripped right out of my chest.

And, well – it wasn't that they didn't like the turn I'd taken with the series, they told me, but they wanted to make sure I was still shooting for a happy ending by the time all of this closed up. I honestly hadn't given much thought to what the ending might look like recently, not since Cameron and I had gotten back together and fixed all the messes we had made. But now –

well, now, I supposed that the story was out in the magazine, and people wanted to see a reflection of the perfect romance that had been written there in the books they sought out from me. It was only fair. It would have been false advertising to do anything else, really.

And so, I decided to take their advice, and try to write a happy ending. It would take my mind off the stress inside my head, at least. I had no idea how I was going to turn the story around from the point that I had left it at and move it to something happier, but perhaps it was time I started thinking about how this tale was going to end for them. After all, now that the story had been reflected in real life, I supposed it was only fair that I think about moving on to something that didn't have a basis in my personal world, right?

I felt like I tried to approach it from every different angle I could. Maybe they could elope? But then, how would I tie up the subplot at the office and with her best friend? No, that wouldn't work, too cheesy. It wouldn't have suited them at all. Could he propose? But that went against something I'd laid out in an earlier chapter – he had never been keen to jump into marriage, and I didn't want to undercut the work I had done on him so far...

Shit. Nothing was easy today. Nothing was making sense to me. Even as I tried to carve out an ending for this story, I felt like I was struggling to think of anything that actually made sense for these characters. Normally, I would have just picked an idea and jumped into that and gone back and changed what I needed to when the time came, but now, it felt like they were connected to Cameron and me, and that meant they contained more than they normally would. These people I had written, they existed in more than just the page, and I wanted to do them justice.

Eventually, I shut down the document I had been trying to work on all this time, and flopped face down on the couch in a total tantrum with myself for not being able to do what I needed to. A happy ending. That was all I needed. A happy ending. And I had gotten one myself – so why couldn't I fill in the gaps in my story?

Maybe it was because there were still questions I was trying to answer in my own life right now. I knew I couldn't rely on Cameron for inspiration as to where to take this story next, but at the same time, I felt like if I could figure things out with him, then the pieces of the story I was trying to write would just fall into place around me. Maybe that was naïve, or maybe I was pinning too much faith on what I wanted from the man I loved. I had no idea.

I took a long bath and ordered something from the deli next door for lunch – I tipped the guy who delivered it an extra ten bucks, in the hopes the universe would see me doing something nice and would give me what I needed in return. But, after lunch, I sat back down at the computer, and I was still coming up with a stone-cold nothing in return for everything I had put out there into the world. How was I meant to make this happen?

I tried to cool myself off, but it didn't do much to help. I just wanted this to be dealt with already. Because I felt that when I put these stories to rest, I could finally move forward with Cameron the way I wanted to. As long as these tales and these characters were still ongoing, I wouldn't be able to leave it behind, but as soon as they were, I could let go and move forward into the real world, with the real man that was more perfect for me than anyone I could ever have written.

If he still wanted to be with me, that was.

The thought crossed my mind, flickering through my head for the briefest moment, and the sound of it in my head was enough to take me by surprise. It was something I hadn't even allowed myself to consider in the time since the shoot had gone ahead, but

I supposed it was relevant, really. Because now that all the drama was done with, there was a chance, a good chance, he had taken a step back and looked at the two of us together and seen something he didn't want to be involved with for the rest of his life.

Shit. And here I was telling him I was in love with him! No wonder he'd had no idea what to say next. If he was having doubts, then the last thing he wanted to hear was my telling him that I loved him, gazing at him with those moon-eyes that spoke to a future I had already planned out for the two of us without an ounce of his input.

Fuck, I needed to get a handle on myself. This was what happened, I supposed, when you really liked someone and you really allowed yourself to fall for them. I couldn't remember the last time this had happened to me, if it had ever happened before at all. There was something dangerous about it, about plunging over the edge and into the sea of emotion, but maybe that was how it was meant to feel. All this time, perhaps that's what I should have been searching for.

I wasn't sure I liked this feeling, of being so out-of-control. It was a wonderful thing when I knew it was returned, but when I was in doubt like this, when I second-guessed myself and left myself wondering if I had gone too far, I didn't know if I was cut out for it.

Suddenly, my phone sprang to life next to me – I answered it at once, not caring if it was just some telemarketer, happy to talk to whoever was on the other end of the line as long as they could get me a little out of my head for the time being.

"Hello?"

"Hi, Alicia," Cameron replied, and my heart felt like it was going to loop-the-loop right out of my chest. I wanted to hear from him, but, at the same time, I had no idea if I was ready to hear everything he had to say to me.

"Yeah?" I replied, prompting him onward, not realizing how sharp and rude I sounded until it was too late.

"I mean, it's good to hear from you," I blurted out, correcting myself. "Is everything okay? Do you need anything?"

"Nothing right now," he replied, sounding amused at how all over the place I was coming off as right now. "But I was hoping you might want to come out for dinner with me tomorrow night?"

"Uh, yeah," I agreed at once. "Yeah, I would love to. Where are we going?"

"I'll pick you up at your apartment at seven," he replied, mysterious as all hell. "Does that work for you?"

"Yeah, of course it does," I replied. "But where are we going?"

"I'd like to keep that as a surprise," he told me, and I bit my lip. My heart felt full all of a sudden, and I could feel that happy little flush to my cheeks. Okay, so maybe I had been a little fast in assuming all of this was done for already, huh?

"I think I can handle that," I replied. "I'll...I guess I'll see you then, okay?"

"See you then," he replied, and with that, he hung up the phone. I stared down at the screen for a moment, unable to keep the smile off my face. I had until tomorrow evening until I got to see him again, got to meet with him in person and the two of us got to be together once more. And I had a feeling he was going to make it one hell of a night to remember.

23

CAMERON

She planted a kiss on my cheek as soon as she rolled into the back of the car beside me, and I took her hand and planted a kiss on her fingers.

"It's so good to see you," I told her, and she beamed at me.

"You too," she replied, and she glanced over at the driver, as though surprised I had gone so all-out.

"Do I get to find out where we're going yet?" she asked with excitement. I slipped my arm around her shoulders and nodded to the driver to keep going.

"Not yet," I replied. "But you will."

"I hope I'm dressed okay for it," she remarked, and she looked down at the little black dress she had thrown on for tonight – she looked gorgeous, like she always did, and I planted a kiss on the corner of her mouth.

"You look perfect," I replied. And I meant it. Not that it would matter much what she looked like, not where we were going, given that it was going to be just us out there for the rest of the night.

I knew I had overdone it a little. I knew I should have played it a little cooler, really. But where was the fun in that, when I could give her something she would never forget? Yes, I could have been all serious and reserved and talked it out with her at her place or something. But I wanted to make sure everything about this night was worthy of one of her books. And I was pretty sure I had put together something she would be proud of.

We arrived outside the beautiful restaurant I had chosen for the night – I was so glad they had agreed to the proposal I'd put forward for this evening, since the food here was always amazing and I knew I wanted her to try it for the first time tonight. It was a classic French place, Michelin-starred, the kind of restaurant most people had to get on a waiting list to even get on a waiting list for. But I had flashed enough cash they had decided it was worth it to allow me to book out the whole place for the two of us.

When we stepped inside, her hand in mine, it took Alicia a moment to figure out what was going on. She looked around, and then furrowed her brow at me.

"Why is it so quiet here?" she asked, and a hostess arrived in front of us to lead us to a small table towards the window at the back. There was a single candle glowing on the white tablecloth, and, as we were guided to our seats, it seemed to sink in to Alicia what the hell was going on.

Her eyes widened and she stared at me for a moment.

"Did you...?" she asked, and I nodded.

"We have this place all to ourselves tonight," I told her. "If you want it, that is."

Her lips parted in total surprise, and she tossed her arms around me and kissed me on the mouth, not caring that the hostess who had led us to our seats was still standing right there next to us.

"Of course I do," she replied, and she brushed her hair back from her face and gazed at me, her eyes shining with this heartfelt delight that made my own heart feel warm.

We took our seats, and she didn't take her eyes off me the whole time, as though she could hardly believe this was actually happening.

"You didn't need to go to all this trouble," she murmured, and I shook my head.

"Maybe I wanted to," I replied. "I thought we could use some time to ourselves to work things out, don't you?"

"But we could have done that at my apartment," she pointed out, and I grinned at her.

"Yes, but I'm dating a romance novelist," I replied. "I'm going to need to put in the effort to prove I'm as romantic as those stories you write, aren't I?"

She giggled and smiled at me.

"I suppose," she agreed. "So, what was it exactly you wanted to talk about?"

I took a deep breath, as the waitress approached with our menus, and I looked down into my pocket where I had the ring box waiting for the right moment to come out and play. There was so much I wanted to say to her, and I really didn't even know where I was meant to start. I just...I wanted to tell her everything that had been running through my head since the moment we'd shared our first kiss, the way everything seemed to have clicked into place as soon as she had come into my life the way that she had. That, even though things had been a mess, they had been the most beautiful mess I had ever been a part of in my life, and I wouldn't have changed a thing about them as long as it brought me to this moment, sitting opposite her at this table, the two of us here, at least, here, where we belonged.

And I knew I had to start at the beginning – I had to start where we had left off. With the words that I should have said to her as soon as I heard them coming out of her mouth.

"Alicia," I murmured to her. "I love you."

Her eyes seemed to glow in the soft light given off by the

candle, and then, for a second, she let them drift shut, as though she was allowing those words to sink into her brain and settle into her head.

"God, you have no idea how much I've wanted to hear that," she told me, her eyes opening once more and looking into mine. "You mean it? I don't want you to feel you have to say it just because I did..."

"I feel it," I promised her. "I know that I do. You know I'm stubborn, I'm not going to come out with anything I don't believe totally."

"Yeah, I do know that," she giggled, the sound of joy on her lips more than I could take for a moment. I felt like my heart was going to swell right on out of my chest. God, I loved her. I loved her so much. I loved her so much it felt like I couldn't contain it for a moment longer, like I needed to stand up on the table and make sure everyone in the damn neighborhood knew what I was thinking.

But, for now, I was just going to share this with her. I had picked out the ring the day before, and I knew it was totally perfect for what I wanted to give to her – it might not have been much, but for now, it was all I was ready for. I knew neither of us wanted to dive into anything too quickly, but this was just a promise – a promise that the two of us could do this, no matter what. That anything the universe threw at us was nothing in comparison to what we felt for one another.

"There's something else I wanted to give you," I admitted, and I reached into my pocket. Her eyes widened as I placed the ring box on the table in front of us, and for a second, it looked as though she was going to start panicking.

"You're not going to propose to me, are you?" she asked at once, and I laughed and shook my head.

"Don't worry, I know you well enough not to spring anything like that on you," I replied, and I popped open the box in front of me and pushed it towards her. Inside, the small silver band, glittering with a perfect emerald, caught the light of the candle.

"This is a promise ring," I explained to her. "And I want you to have it. I know we've been through a lot these last few weeks, and I know I wouldn't have been able to get through it if I had been with anyone other than you."

"I don't think I would have wanted to get through it if I'd had to put up with it with anyone other than you," she remarked, and I grinned and shook my head in amusement.

"Yeah, something like that," I agreed. "It's...I know it's a lot. And I know we still have a lot to figure out between us, trust me. But I want to give ourselves the time to work it out. I want to be with you, properly. And I want you to know I'm not going anywhere. I don't care how long it takes us to work all of this out, I'm going to be here, right here with you, to make it happen."

She looked down at the ring again, and, slowly, she reached for it and slipped it over her finger. She held her hand out in front of her and took a long look at the jewel on her finger. I knew it was as good as a yes, but I needed to hear those words out of her mouth before I could believe it.

"Yes," she breathed, finally, her gaze shifting to me once more. "Yes. All of it. I mean...I know we have a lot to work out, but I want to try this, Cameron. Because I love you."

"I love you too," I replied, and the flow of the words between us felt so natural it was hard to believe I hadn't said them back to her the first time she had spoken them to me. I leaned over the table, kissed her lips, and then took the hand with a ring on it and pressed my mouth to the small silver band.

"I think I'm ready to eat now," she murmured, and I laughed.

"I did promise you dinner," I conceded, and I reached for a menu. Honestly, it took me a moment to actually be able to focus on all the dishes in front of me – I was still so caught up in everything that had just happened, I had almost forgotten that my stomach had been growling when we had arrived here.

But we ordered a selection, and soon, the delicious food was being brought out for us. I was so happy I could have turned to the wait staff and told them everything that had just happened between us. I knew it was a long shot, going all out and putting in this much effort and everything, but it was perfect. Really, truly, and totally perfect. I loved her, and I wanted her to see that. And I knew now that she understood it, the way I needed her to.

24

ALICIA

"Come here," I murmured to him, as I pulled him over the door to my apartment and into my arms. I held my hand out for a moment, admiring the ring that was glistening on my finger, and he kissed my neck and smiled against my skin.

"Okay, you're going to have to actually pay attention to me instead of that damn ring," he told me, his mouth pressed against my ear. "Or else I'm going to have to take that thing off you."

"Hmm, good luck with that," I purred back to him, as his mouth skimmed over my neck and up to meet my lips. His tongue sank into my mouth, and I kicked the door shut behind us and let myself get lost to him once and for all.

I couldn't believe how perfect this night had been. He had put in so much effort, hiring out the restaurant and making sure I had all the space I needed to make the choice he wanted me to make. Talk about romance; I wasn't sure I could have come up with something half as perfect as that if I had been trying, and I was meant to be the one who wrote this stuff for a living.

I didn't care about that now. All I cared about was having him and making him mine, showing him in every way I could that I wanted him and that this had been the right choice for him to make.

"You're perfect," he murmured, pulling back for a moment to look into my eyes. It seemed like he was looking at the most beautiful thing in the world; I never wanted to forget how this moment felt, in the first flush of this love for him, knowing that he loved me back and everything was the way it should have been between us.

"Come show me," I breathed back, and he grinned and scooped me up off the ground. I giggled and hung on to him as he carried me through to the apartment and towards my bedroom. He was so strong. How had I never noticed how strong he was before we started all of this? I couldn't get over how perfect he was, how beautiful he was and how much he loved me; that I had this man all to myself, and nobody was ever going to take that away from me. He had put a ring on my finger to promise me that, and I wasn't going to let anything else get in the way.

He tossed me down on to the bed and pounced on top of me – I hooked my arms tight around him and pulled him down so I could feel his full weight on top of me, as his mouth found mine once more and I tasted him again. We had shared a bottle of wine at dinner, and I could taste the sharp, sweet flavor on his lips, the two of us drunk on one another.

"I love you," he murmured in my ear again, as his hands traveled up beneath my skirt, gripping my thighs.

"I love you, too," I told him, and I felt a surge of hopeless lust for him – it was the strangest thing I had ever felt, this distinct want that came from knowing he loved me. That emotional connection, it ran deeper than anything I had ever felt before, and it was more powerful than anything I had ever felt.

I reached down and unzipped his pants, sliding my hand over his underwear and squeezing his cock beneath his boxers.

"You know this is mine now," I purred to him playfully, and he kissed my neck again, making my heart pick up in my chest.

"Oh, yeah?" he replied. "Prove it."

And with that, I decided I would do just that. I flipped over on him, so I was on top for a change – looking down at him, at his gorgeousness all laid out underneath me. I bit my lip and let out a happy little sigh.

"You like what you see?" he asked, and I smiled and nodded as I began to undo the shirt he had worn for our special dinner together. I could feel his heart beating hard under his skin, and I shifted back and forth on his hardening cock, enjoying the way it stirred at my touch.

"Mmm," I purred, and I pushed his shirt open to show him off to me. I loved this – I loved him. There was something just so special about being with him, about being with a man I loved so much, about knowing he loved me back. I had been with plenty of men before, but there was something about being with him that made it feel so different.

I reached his pants, pushed them down, and his hands came to my waist as though he wanted to push me down on top of him already. But I was going to make him wait. I was going to take my sweet-ass time in getting there, and he was just going to have to wait.

I stripped him down, making sure to trail my fingers or my lips over every exposed inch of skin as I showed him off – in the dim light of the bedroom, it was hard to think about anything else but him, hard to believe there was anything else outside of this room right now. There was a world beyond these walls, but I didn't know anything about it. I didn't want to know, either. I just needed him, and the rest of the universe could wait.

By the time that he was naked, I was still wearing my dress, even my heels, and that's the way I wanted to keep it. I took his cock in my hand and stroked it a few times, watching the tension that appeared in his jaw when I caressed him in this way. He let out a groan and tipped his head back into my pillow.

"How long are you going to make me wait?" he asked. I bit my lip. Well, I supposed it was only fair that I give in. I reached beneath my dress and pulled my panties aside, and, slowly, taking my time, I lowered myself down on top of his cock and took him inside of me once and for all.

"God," I groaned, tipping my head back and letting the feeling rush through me. The sensation was glorious, so satisfying, everything I had been waiting for since I had dragged him back through that door.

"Fuck," he breathed back, and he reached out to grab hold of my hips, pushing me back and forth on top of him to let his full length drive inside of me.

"You look so good like that," he murmured, his eyes tracing down my whole body as though he wished he could take a bite out of me right there and then. I reached down and pulled the dress to the side so he could see him inside of me, and he groaned with pleasure as he saw the sight of us together.

He sat up and wrapped his arms around me and pushed himself deeper inside of me – his mouth was on my throat again, his hands pushing down the straps of my dress so he could kiss all over my shoulders and my neck and my collar. He was so warm, his breath hot on my skin, and I ran my fingers through his hair, cradling his head close to me. He was thrusting up into me, over and over again, driving himself deep until all I could feel was the way that he felt, the way we felt when we were together.

"You feel so good," I murmured to him, pulling back and clasping his face in my hands so I could gaze into his eyes. They were pinned to me, like he was drinking me in, taking the pleasure right from mine and letting it build on his until we were both pushing towards the edge of the release we needed so badly.

My hips were slithering back and forth on top of him, and I closed my eyes and pressed my forehead to his so I could feel his breath on mine and get where I needed to go. I could see my ring glinting on my finger, a reminder of the commitment he had made to me, and I felt that pushing me towards the edge.

"I love you so much," he gasped to me, his voice cracking around the edges, and his hands clasped my face so the two of us were just staring at each other, moving together, pushing each other towards the edge we needed to reach.

"I love you, too," I breathed back. And then, finally, I felt it hit me, that rush of pleasure consume me, growing from between my legs and flooding through my system. I didn't take my eyes off his, and he didn't either, and the two of us came in the same moment, his cock twitching inside of me as he filled me with his seed. I rocked slowly back and forth on top of him, squeezing the last that I could get out of him, determined to enjoy every drop of it. He kissed me again, softly, inhaling deeply as he did so, as though he was breathing in every inch of me that he could.

Slowly, he lifted me off of him, and I sank down onto the bed and flopped back with delight, staring at the ceiling and smiling broadly. I knew I should have taken off my dress and my heels before I messed up the bed, but I didn't care. I was just too sated to think about moving an inch. And he knew it.

"Well, I think you made giving you that ring worth it," he joked, and I lifted my head and raised my eyebrows at him.

"I beg your pardon?" I replied, and he reached for me and kissed me on the thigh. I closed my eyes and let this little rush of happiness take control of me. I adored this man, I really did. He had made tonight perfect, made sure that the first time we said those words to each other had really meant something.

"You're perfect," he assured me. "I'm not going anywhere. I want you to know that. The ring is meant to promise that, right?"

"Yes, it does," I agreed, and I held it out in front of me and gazed at it for a moment. Then, it hit me.

"What are you smiling about?" he asked, lifting his head to look at me. I didn't even notice the big grin that had spread all over my face.

"I think you've just given me the perfect ending for my series," I replied, and he beamed at me.

"Hey, and here I was thinking I would never be romantic enough to meet your standards," he joked. I shook my head at him.

"How on earth could that be?" I pointed out. "He's based on you. You had to be the most romantic person I'd ever met, right?"

"I suppose you have a point," he agreed, and he kissed my thigh again. Propping his chin up on my leg, he just looked at me for a moment, as though marveling that this was really happening. And I reached out and ran my fingers through his hair, my fingertips trailing down his cheek and his jaw and over his stubble. My best friend. My lover. Everything I had ever wanted. And he was all mine.

EPILOGUE
CAMERON

"Are you ready to go?" I asked, checking my watch and glancing at the door nervously. Alicia emerged from the bedroom, one hand on her lower back, and let out a groan.

"Are you sure we really have to go?" she asked me, and I went over to her and put an arm around her shoulders.

"You know we do," I reminded her gently. "But it's going to be over soon."

"And at least your mom is going to be at this one," she replied. "She always keeps me entertained. Bitching about everyone at the company…"

I laughed.

"I thought you were meant to hate your in-laws," I pointed out, and she shrugged.

"Maybe that'll change when we actually get engaged," she pointed out.

"Maybe," I agreed. "Hey, you ready to go? I don't want to be late."

"Yeah, the sooner we get there, the sooner we can leave," she grumbled, but I knew she was just kidding. I kissed her on the top of the head and opened the door, and the two of us stepped outside to head down to the party we had organized specifically for this very occasion.

I couldn't believe that six months had passed since the day I had given her the ring – well, thereabouts, anyway. I measured the time we had officially gotten together by the length of her pregnancy, even though we weren't quite sure on when that had started. There had been a whole lot of hooking up and fooling around in those early days, and it seemed like we hadn't been as careful as we might have been, and, well, when she started feeling ill in the mornings, I supposed we both knew where it was going.

It had been a shock, of course, but in the best way possible. We had talked about the future a lot – about where we wanted to live, when we wanted to get married, where we planned to raise a family and when we planned to do it. It wasn't even a question of if it would happen – why would we need to think about that, when everything seemed so set in stone for the two of us as it was?

"Are we really going to do this?" Alicia had asked me, when we had been at the doctor's, getting the very first scan for our baby. Her eyes were shining, and I could tell she was nervous, but I knew she wanted this. From the moment she had taken the first test and the two of us had found out the truth, I knew this was what she wanted.

"We are," I promised her, and I lifted her hand to my mouth, a little gesture that had grown into habit since I had given her the ring. I closed my eyes and kissed her finger, kissed the gem that promised her to me, and then met her gaze once more.

"I can't believe this is really happening," she murmured. I shook my head, still kind of marveling at it too.

"Me neither," I replied. "But it is."

"I thought I needed a new project after I finished the books," she joked. "But I didn't think it would be...well, something like this..."

"Sometimes you've got to branch out of your comfort zone a little, right?" I joked back, and she laughed, and the doctor stepped back into the room and stared at both of us for a moment as though trying to figure out what the hell happened to be so funny. I managed to contain the smirk that wanted to come out of me, and we went back to listening to everything we would need to know about the rest of our pregnancy.

It was a hell of a lot to take in all at once, but I did my best to wrap my head around it and to keep up with everything that needed to be done to make sure Alicia had the most perfect pregnancy that she could. And that started with moving her into my apartment – we agreed that my place was the one we wanted to live in, given it had much more space and a faster internet connection so she could carry on with her writing, and soon enough, her trinkets and clothes and makeup were strewn all about the place, like flags claiming the territory as her own.

"Now I remember why I didn't want to live with you again," I had teased her, as I cleaned up some of her clothes left strewn on the end of the bed.

"What, because you knew you wouldn't be able to resist having me around without making a move?" she shot back, propping her feet up on a pillow at the end of the bed.

"Something like that," I replied, planting a kiss on the top of her feet. "You want me to get you a cup of tea?"

"I thought you'd never ask," she agreed, and she picked up her book and flicked through it to find the page she had been reading at last.

That was something else she had brought into my house – books. Not just her own collection, but the ones she wrote, too. She had finally finished up the series she had written about the two of us. Well, okay, she might not have meant it, but there was no doubt it reflected our relationship. And for the final scene she had even drawn on the dinner I'd taken her out for the first time that I'd told her I loved her; people loved it, and it had even wound up on a couple of best-seller lists. I was so proud of her, so proud she had proved she was such a force to be reckoned with in the industry. And I couldn't wait to read what she would write next. She had even dedicated the last book to me, and she promised the next would be for our baby – well, depending on how appropriate the subject matter was, of course.

And my whole family just loved her. My mom, especially, had practically been dancing around in triumph when I had told her the two of us were together for good, and I was pretty sure she was going to burst with excitement when I let her know we were going to have a baby. I was worried she might try to stick her nose in more than it was wanted, but she was careful and considerate and kind. She had been a huge help to the both of us, helping us pick out stuff for the nursery, and even consoling Alicia when she was having some anxiety about somehow doing something wrong in all of this.

Matt, too, had actually taken the time to get to know Alicia. It wasn't something that I had anticipated – I didn't know what I expected to happen between us now everything with Adrienne was done with, but he had made a real effort to be part of my life.

"I know that I fucked up," he had told me, bluntly, over a couple of beers after work when I had outright come and ask him what was going through his head.

"But we made a good thing together," he went on. "And I don't want to lose that. And besides, you – you're still one of the only people who's stuck around through all of this shit. I figure if we can make it through that, we can make it through anything."

"I guess you have a point," I agreed. Maybe the beers were helping, but I was feeling a little more charitable towards him than I had before. The more time that passed since his indiscretion with Adrienne, the more time he put into proving he never planned to hurt me like that again, the easier I was finding it to come back around to trusting him once more. I knew it was going to take a while before I got there for good, but for now, I would take what I could get. He was right – we made a good thing together, and there was no point in tossing all of that away when things were beginning to fade into the rearview mirror.

He had been a big part of helping to organize this baby shower – in fact, as soon as he had found out about the pregnancy, he had insisted on doing everything he could to make things as easy for me as he possibly could. He seemed to accept that the two of us were going to need as much help as we could get in making this work, and Matt was quick to put in place everything I would need to have a few months of paternity leave as soon as the little one had come along.

We didn't know what gender the baby was going to be – the doctor had offered to find out for us, but we had decided to leave it until we got to hold it in our arms and see for ourselves. We didn't want to know anything about it that it couldn't introduce all by itself.

And now, we were going down to the baby shower that was being thrown to celebrate our little one coming into the world at large. Mom had insisted we keep it in the building where my apartment was, not wanting to drag Alicia any further out of her way than she had to go, and I was more than happy to go along with it. She knew pregnancy better than I did, and besides, it would mean the two of us could make a quick escape when the time came.

"You sure you're feeling up to this?" I asked Alicia, as the two of us stepped into the elevator to take us down to the party. She smiled at me and nodded.

"Yeah, I really am," she replied. "I was just kidding back

there, really. It's so sweet that everyone has gone out of their way for me like this. Besides, I'm not going to turn down the chance to talk about how great our kid is, am I?"

"You're going to be a totally insufferable mother," I teased her. "You're totally going to be talking about how your kid is the best at everything, aren't you?"

"Well, yes," she replied. "But the difference for me is that our kid actually *will* be the best at everything."

"You make a fair point," I laughed, and, as the doors slid shut in front of us, I leaned over and planted a kiss on her cheek. Her eyes softened and she smiled at me, leaning herself up against me as though glad, for a moment, to have the chance to take the weight off her feet.

"I love you," I told her, and she closed her eyes for a moment.

"I love you, too," she replied, and I slid my hand over her belly to feel the roundness of her bump beneath my hand. I couldn't believe that this woman contained so much – my future, my past, my legacy, my family. I was more grateful to her for everything she was doing than she would ever know, and I intended to spend the rest of my life making sure that I told her it in every way I possibly could.

The doors slid open in front of us, at the floor where the party was taking place, and she wound her fingers into mine.

"Into the breach?" she asked, and I nodded.

"I'm right behind you," I promised her. And, as the two of us walked out together, I knew that I meant it. And would keep meaning it. For as long as I lived.

MORE BOOKS BY JESSIE COOKE

Just like Grey Novels

Just like Grey Boxsets

Just like Grey Singles

Hot Mess - A One-of-a-Kind Romantic Comedy Action Adventure unlike anything you've ever read!

All My Books including MC Romance and Bad Boys at JessieCooke.com

Copyright © Jessie Cooke

All rights reserved.

No part of this book may be reproduced in any form or by any electronic or mechanical means, including information storage and retrieval systems, without written permission from the author, except for the use of brief quotations in a book review.

License.

This book is available exclusively on Amazon.com. If you found this book for free or from a site other than Amazon.com country specific website it means the author was not compensated and you have likely obtained the book through an unapproved distribution channel.

Acknowledgements

This book is a work of fiction. The names, characters, places and events are products of the writer's imagination or have been used fictitiously and are not to be construed as real. Any resemblance to people, living or dead, actual events, locales or organizations is entirely coincidental.

Printed in Great Britain
by Amazon